Also by Edward D. Hoch:

The Judges of Hades
The Transvection Machine
The Spy and the Thief
City of Brass
The Fellowship of the Hand
The Frankenstein Factory
The Thefts of Nick Velvet

AUTHOR'S   NOTE

Because many living people and actual places are mentioned by
name in the novel that follows, it might be well to point out that the
names of characters, places and companies listed below are wholly fic-
titious, and derive from no real person or place.

Amalgamated Broadcasting Co.	WJON Radio
Irma Black	*Manhattan Magazine*
Tom and Rick Clancy	Dick McMullen
Claxton Trust Company	Mrs. Phillipps
Schuyler Craig	Betty Rafferty
Ross Craigthorn	Arthur Rowe
Harry Fox	Skinny Simon
Detective George	Mary Sweeney
Barney Hamet	Mr. Tyron
Frank Jesset	Susan Veldt
Victor Jones	Max Winters
June, Nebraska	

EDWARD D. HOCH
THE SHATTERED RAVEN

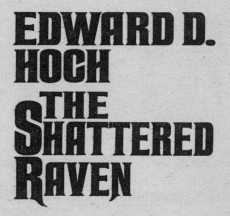

DALE BOOKS
New York

For my mother
. . . and for Patricia

Copyright © 1969, 1978 by Edward D. Hoch

All Rights Reserved.

Library of Congress Catalog Number: 77-93940

ISBN 0-89559-012-3

Printed in the United States of America

Chapter One

VICTOR JONES

Victor Jones felt good that morning.

It was the day after Easter, and Manhattan was bathed in a sunshine comparatively rare for this early in the spring. From his window he could see strollers far below along the street, bound for nowhere, asking nothing, only breathing in the deep fresh air of the day and perhaps smiling to each other as they passed.

He felt good, that is, until the morning mail was spread on the desk before him. Then he saw the letter at once, addressed to him in a vaguely familiar hand, and bearing the return address of Amalgamated Broadcasting Company. He knew, before opening the envelope, that it was a letter from Ross Craigthorn.

Ross Craigthorn—a name from the past, a name he rarely thought of any more in connection with his own well-ordered life. Of course Craigthorn could be seen on television nightly; his half-hour news commentary for Amalgamated reached more homes than Huntley or Brinkley or Cronkite or any of the others. But that was something different, something remote, as when he occasionally saw Craigthorn's handsome face across the room at a crowded party to which they'd both been invited. The fact remained that they had not spoken to each other, nor communicated in any way, for some twenty-two years.

And now, after all that time, this letter had come. He slit open the envelope and pulled out the two sheets of paper. The letter had been neatly typed, but it was obvious that Ross had done it himself on his personal machine. This was not the sort of letter to be entrusted to curious secretaries.

Dear Victor, it began. *Dear Victor*. He hadn't seen that salutation in twenty-two years.

Dear Victor,

Perhaps you will be surprised to hear from me after all these years, and you may be more surprised that I am addressing you by your real name. The envelope, of course, bears another name, but to me you will always be Victor Jones.

Why am I writing you after all these years? I think at one time, just after it happened, I swore I would never see you again or speak your name or do anything that might remind me of that awful past.

But now, Victor, something has happened which brings it all back, which forces me to an action I never thought I would have to take. You see, Victor, I have been contacted by Irma.

Yes, Irma—Irma Black. You remember Irma. She was there. She saw it all. Saw us. Knew our names. Our names at that time, anyway. And now Irma is in Manhattan. She has found me, of course, because my name did not really change that much, and my face is on television every night.

Irma Black has contacted me and asked for one hundred thousand dollars. It is not a small sum, believe me, despite what you might have read in the trade press about my new contract. It is, in fact, too large a sum for me to think of paying. For Irma Black it would only be the first of many sums—many hundreds of thousands of dollars—and surely she knows what she could do to me, to my reputation. And that is why she asks so large an amount.

It is paradoxical, I suppose, Victor, to think that if I were a factory worker or a garbage collector the sin of our past would be worth no money to anyone. It is only the fame that has been thrust upon me which makes it a valuable sin, suddenly valuable to people like Irma Black.

I will not pay the blackmail, Victor. I will not pay one cent to the woman. And so I am left with a sticky alternative. She can break the story in any number of columns around town, blacken my name, perhaps ruin my reputation. I cannot allow her to do that.

The only explanation, the only path that seems open to me, is to beat her to the punch. The statute of limitations has run out on our crime, as you know. I feel that if I go before the public and tell them what I did—what we did —on that night so long ago, perhaps—just perhaps—I can convince them it was a youthful folly. I can beg their forgiveness, throw myself on their mercy, and keep my position in the broadcast world. Perhaps.

In any event, it is the only course open to me and it is one which I must take. That is why I am writing to you at this time, Victor, because of course I cannot reveal my crime without revealing our crime. I will have to tell your part in it, and even if I do not identify you by your present name, I fear the identity which you have assumed will not long remain a mystery.

I'm sorry to have to do this—to drag you into it. You with your family, with your fine reputation in the field. But I have no choice, as you can see. I did feel, however, that this letter was called for, that something must be said before I took this action. Feel free to phone me, Victor, if there is anything you want to say, but be advised that my decision is irrevocable. The truth must come out. I hope you will agree with this course of action, and I beg your forgiveness in advance for any trouble and heartbreak it may cause you.

Yours for an honest future,
Ross Craigthorn

Victor Jones finished reading the letter and sat for a long time staring at it on the desk before him. Then, lighting a cigarette to calm his nerves, he read it over once more from the beginning.

When he had finished the second time, he picked up the telephone, remembered he did not know the number of Amalgamated Broadcasting, and set down the receiver again while he consulted the directory. He dialed the number with a hand remarkably steady and asked to speak with Ross Craighthorn, just as any businessman might. There was some delay. Finally a secretary came on the wire. "Mr. Craigthorn is recording at the moment. Could he return your call?"

"No. No." Victor Jones said. "I will phone him again a bit later." He hung up and smoked another cigarette, stared out the window and wondered what in hell he was going to do with his life.

An hour later he managed to reach Ross Craigthorn. The voice on the other end was just a bit surprised. "Well—Victor, isn't it? Is that the name I should call you?"

"I received your letter this morning, Ross."

A grunt on the other end. "I thought I'd made it clear what the situation was, but I'm glad you called, nevertheless. It's a difficult thing—difficult for me—difficult for you. It'll be difficult for our families as well."

Victor Jones was staring at nothing. "You can't go through with this, Ross. The past is dead. Buried."

"Of course it is, but that foolish woman is trying to bring it to life again."

"How much money does she want, Ross?"

"I told you in the letter. A hundred thousand now, and who knows how much in the future? It can't be paid. It won't be paid."

For just a moment Victor Jones was back—back into decades of time. To the place where it had all begun with the two of them.

"Doesn't our friendship mean anything to you, Ross?"

"Of course it does, Victor. It's meant something to me for all these years, even though we don't see each other any more. You've been successful and so have I."

Victor interrupted. "You're far the more successful of the two of us."

"Then I have the most to lose, haven't I? I have the most to lose by getting up and telling people what happened all those years ago. If I'm willing to risk it, Victor, you should be too."

Victor Jones tightened his grip on the receiver. "I'm not

4

willing to risk it, Ross. I'm not! I'm not! You can't tell them what happened! You can't bring me into it."

"I'll try to keep you out of it, of course. I'll try to be vague about your identity. Perhaps they won't guess—and perhaps they will. There's no way of telling the story without leaving hints. It can't be helped. This woman is on my back. It's the only way I know to get rid of her, short of murder."

"Maybe you should consider that, Ross."

Craigthorn laughed. "Always the kidder, Victor. Didn't you get us into enough trouble twenty-two years ago?"

"Then you're really going through with it?"

"I am."

"When?"

"Funny thing! You know—of course, you know—that I've always read mystery novels. You did too, back in those days. This group, the Mystery Writers of America, is presenting me with an award as the Reader of the Year. I guess that I've mentioned a few times on television that I read them, even reviewed a couple on my program. The dinner is at the Biltmore, a week from Friday. Funny thing—speaking to all those mystery writers, editors and such. A lot of people go to the dinner. Perhaps you'll be there yourself, although I wouldn't want to embarrass you needlessly. Anyway, it seems like a good opportunity to tell the story. I think they'd be a sympathetic audience and I think the press would break it in the right way."

Victor Jones said nothing for a moment. Then, finally, he commented "That's a damnable thing to do, Ross. Don't you know. . . ?"

Craigthorn interrupted him. "I can't talk any more now, Victor. My decision has been made. I'm sorry. I'll try to keep you out of it as best I can. Goodbye!"

There was a click and the line went dead, and Victor Jones was left holding the receiver. He hung up slowly, then sat pondering the desk calendar before him. Yes . . . he already had a note that the MWA dinner was a week from Friday. A coincidence of sorts, he supposed, that their paths should come together in exactly this way.

He turned back to his typewriter and started to write a

piece he'd been trying to do all week. But nothing came to his churning mind.

Ross Craigthorn was going to talk. What to do? What to do? He pondered that for the better part of an hour before he decided, quite suddenly, and with no second thoughts, that he would have to murder Ross Craigthorn.

Chapter Two

SUSAN VELDT

For Susan Veldt it had all begun on a snowy morning back in January when she'd come to work late because the Fifth Avenue buses were piled up in a traffic jam at 42nd Street. Long ago she had wished for a subway beneath Fifth Avenue, and in the summer she avoided the problem by taking the Sixth Avenue and walking a block, but on a morning like this, she was not about to brave the slushy snow that collected at every corner. It was the bus for her, and when the bus was late, she was late, too.

She lived uptown, in a section that many people considered fancy, facing Central Park with a good view of the zoo. It was a fine apartment, sublet to her by a college friend who was spending a year in Europe, and who came from a family with money. Susan was glad to have the apartment and thankful for the view of the park, even though an occasional lion's roar drifted up to her room on the nights when she slept with the window open.

This morning, though, the silence of the snow was everywhere, and even the animals seemed to be smothered in it. She saw them drifting lazily in their snowy cages as she waited for the bus, and when it finally came, she boarded it and settled in for the long trip down to 22nd Street and the far-from-palatial offices of *Manhattan* magazine.

Susan Veldt was a staff writer for *Manhattan*, a job that paid her a mild eighty-two hundred dollars a year but carried with it a certain amount of prestige in New York literary circles. *Manhattan* had been born out of the foggy dreams of its publisher and editor, Arthur Rowe, a brilliant man out of the midwest, whose every project seemed to bring with it the unceasing flow of monetary profit.

Susan had heard of the founding of *Manhattan* the previous summer, and when the critics sneered at another Gotham-oriented magazine along with *The New Yorker* and *New York* and *Cue* and the rest, she set off for the downtown offices to see what it was all about.

Arthur Rowe, bespectacled, thin of hair and chomping a pipe between yellow teeth, impressed her immediately. He looked like an editor should look, and talked like an editor should talk. He pointed a pencil at her and told her to get to work that first day, and she'd been working ever since.

The magazine was a weekly, with Susan doing a by-lined article every second or third week. She had explored, among other topics, the Central Park Zoo, the plans for a nuclear power plant in Queens, Mayor Lindsay's latest walking tours, the unemployed show folk of Broadway, and the creeps of 42nd Street. She had, in six or seven short months, covered the city from one end to another. Still, Arthur Rowe always managed to produce new assignments for her, and this snowy January morning was no exception.

"I've got a great idea, Sue!" he said, lighting up the pipe. "You're going to do a series for us called *It Happens Every Spring*."

"Baseball?" she asked, looking a bit askance.

"No baseball. There was a baseball movie of that title back in the fifties, with Paul Douglas. Remember him? He's dead now. No, it's going to be about the awards business. The awards business here in Manhattan. Look at this—the New York Film Critics just gave out their awards, and some other critics' group, too. It happens all the time. Especially, it happens in New York in the spring. You're going to cover all the dinners and all the banquets—all the ceremonies—and then you'll write me a nice series on them."

"Straight or funny?" she asked, chewing at the eraser tip of her pencil.

"Use your own judgment. I think more funny than straight—a little bit of satire—a little bit of needle. You know the sort of thing. Make like you're working for *The New Yorker* on this one."

She chuckled and got out her notebook. "When do I start?"

"First I want a list of them—how many there are, which ones we should cover. We'll have another meeting on it in a couple of days. Meantime, work on the research."

"How about the Oscars? Are they included?"

"Oscars are Hollywood. This is Manhattan. No Oscars. You don't get a free trip to the Coast, Susan."

She sighed and made a note on her pad, and went out.

For Susan Veldt, that was the beginning of it.

The next meeting actually took place a full week later, because Arthur Rowe had been called to the printers in Albany, where they were always having indecipherable problems with web offset presses. He returned gloomy and full of curse words for the men who ran that end of the business, then settled into his black leather armchair and stared at her as if he had no idea in the world what brought her to his sanctum.

"What's up, Susan?" he asked.

"Well, what's *up* is that you wanted me to cover those awards—the Manhattan awards. You know."

"Oh, yes. Do you have a list of them?"

"Here," she sighed, starting off with number one. "The Grammy Awards, little miniature . . ."

He interrupted immediately. "Little miniature is redundant. Susan, I'm going to make a writer out of you if it kills me, and you too."

"All right. All right," she said, agreeing, happy to see that he was relaxing. "The Grammy Awards, given for the best records of the year in various categories. The awards are presented at a banquet around the end of February. There's a television show that follows later, but the banquet is the thing to cover."

"Good," he told her, making a note on the big yellow pad before him. "Next?"

"The National Book Awards, second week in March. Very, very literary. Lots of speeches, including usually a blast at the war or the way things are being run in Washington."

"Good." He made a note of it, then looked up for her next entry.

"The Oscars come in early April, but we're not covering those. Then we skip to about mid-April for the Tony Awards. You know, the Antoinette Perry, American Theatre Wing."

"Right. Then where are we?"

"Usually about a week later, the New York Drama Critics give a ..."

He interrupted. "We're too late for the Film Critics. We'd better leave off the Drama Critics too or we'll get a rhubarb going about favoritism. The Tony Awards will cover that end of it."

"Right, Boss." She liked to call him that—when the mood was light. "That's just one less article I have to write. Let's see ..." She bit at the pencil again, wishing she had a cigarette. She didn't really smoke a great deal, but one would have tasted good just then. Of course Rowe kept some on his desk. He even occasionally smoked one when he ran out of pipe tobacco, but she didn't want to ask right now and disturb his genial disposition.

"In late April, we have the Edgar Awards."

"The what?" he asked.

"*Edgar*. For Edgar Allan Poe. They're given by the Mystery Writers of America for the best detective novel, short story, movie, television show, things like that."

"Sounds good," he said. "I think I've read something about them somewhere. I'm not much of a mystery buff myself, though."

She hurried on. "Early May—around the first week, the Pulitzer Prizes are given up at Columbia University."

"That's one we want," he said.

"Then, I think we could wind up about mid-May with the Emmy Awards—the television things, you know. They

10

have a joint ceremony, in New York and Hollywood."

"Right. How many does that make altogether?"

"Well, let's see. We have the Grammys and the National Book Awards and the Tonys and the Edgars. That's four . . . and the Pulitzers and the Emmys—which would be six."

"Six is a good number for a series. Let's make it six. We might decide on a lead article or a concluding article summarizing the whole thing, but figure on six for now. Get at your typewriter and start working!"

She got at her typewriter later that afternoon, plugging away at what would be an initial article, or at least the rationale for the series as it existed in her own mind.

It happens every spring, she began, picking out the letters on her electric typewriter. *The awards business is big business because it's the sort of business that encourages other business. Whenever something wins an award in any field of the arts, be it a movie or a book or a television show or a phonograph record or a play or just about anything, it generally means increased grosses, increased sales, increased customers—more money to the author or the producer or whoever it is involved in the thing. Perhaps the most famous awards of this sort are the Oscars and they are given in Hollywood, but the remainder of the awards business is centered in New York and it is big business, as I have said. It is a business that runs all year round and reaches its climax on the island of Manhattan in the spring, where no less than six major sets of awards are given out to the happy participants. The awards are given at televised events with lavish banquets, or just plain semi-private meetings, and the news generally appears in* The New York Times *and other papers the following morning. Sometimes the names of the winners leak out in advance, but generally it's kept a well-guarded secret until the actual night of the event.*

In this series of articles, I intend to take you to these events—six of them, at least—being held in Manhattan this spring. I think you'll enjoy the experience. I know I will.

Susan was twenty-seven years old, a sharp-tongued

young lady with blonde hair and a good figure. She'd been writing successfully ever since college—poems, even one or two short stories published in the women's magazines. But her biggest success had come with an exposé piece she'd done for a now defunct morning newspaper, on a private club up in the Bronx. That had made her name around New York.

She'd always told her friends—and even her father, when he protested about her writing career—that a girl with looks *and* brains could get further than anyone else in Manhattan. She was proving it because she had both. Some called her the sexiest magazine writer in Manhattan, and perhaps that wasn't very far from wrong. Unfortunately, with Susan herself, *writer* came before *sexy*. Considering the fact of her twenty-seven years, and the number of eligible men on the island of Manhattan, it remained a dour fact of life that she had never married—and had slept with only two men in all those years. One had been a college senior, who practically raped her after a drunken fraternity party. The other was a silk-shirted Manhattan ad man, who didn't even remember her name afterward.

It had given her a sort of displeasure about the whole thing, the whole game, whatever you call it—and she was deciding at about this point in her young life that she could take men or leave them alone. It didn't matter a bit to her, either way.

She covered the Grammy Awards dinner at the end of February, jotting down notes between courses and glancing around at the top recording executives and the young long-haired singing stars. It was an experience, to say the least, and she wrote a good article on it. Arthur Rowe was pleased. He even raised her salary ten dollars a week.

The National Book Awards was a bit different. Most of the writers tended to have beards that year, for some reason, and they looked at her without really seeing her. All except one young hippie poet, who made a half-hearted attempt to seduce her at the bar. Then they went in and listened to the fellow who'd won the novel award bubble through a prepared speech and thank everyone in sight, from his agent through his publisher to his mother. Susan felt it was a discouraging lack of professionalism on his part, and she said so in her article.

Things picked up a bit with the Tony Awards. She'd sat at home the night of the Oscar presentation, her eyes glued to the television screen, and it was amazing to see how the Tony show copied some of the best and worst features of the Oscar. It was held in one of the larger Shubert Alley theatres on a Sunday night, so everyone could attend. And again the television cameras were very much in evidence. She liked seeing the stars, and they had a bigger line-up of names than the other two awards ceremonies. Her mother would have enjoyed overhearing her little after-curtain chat with Robert Goulet and Carol Channing.

The Tony Awards came the Sunday after Easter that year—only five days before the annual dinner of the Mystery Writers of America. That was why she found herself on the street that sunny Monday morning, seeking out the second-floor headquarters of MWA on 48th Street. It was to be a big day in the life of Susan Veldt. It was to be the day she met Barney Hamet.

Chapter Three

BARNEY HAMET

Betty Rafferty, executive secretary of Mystery Writers of America, looked up from her typewriter and called across the room to the tall, husky young man by the window. "Barney, what should I tell Max out in Los Angeles?"

Barney Hamet turned and stared at her. "What's the problem with Max?"

"He's not planning to come east for the Awards Dinner, and he's our novel winner."

Barney walked over to the desk and glanced down at the tentative seating list for Friday night's affair. No, Max Winters was definitely not on it, and that was odd. He'd made every dinner since Barney joined MWA, and there had been no thought that he'd miss this one.

Although the awards were not announced until Friday, and were kept more or less secret, Betty and Barney and a handful of others already knew the winners' names. Max Winters had won the novel award for his medium-best-seller, *The Fox Hunt*, a fairly successful attempt to blend the detective story with the mainstream novel. Although he was one of six nominees, all of them worthy, the novel committee had wasted little time in picking Max's book as the winner. Barney knew Max and he was pleased with the choice.

Now, pondering the dinner list, he felt a pang of discontent. "What do we usually do in cases like this? Don't we generally notify the winner and break the news to him in advance—tell him he's won? It's always good to have as many of the winners as possible at the dinner."

"That's been the practice in the past," Betty agreed. "If there's travel involved, if the person isn't planning to attend, we do sometimes tell him that he's won."

"All right," Barney said. "Get a letter off to him over my signature and drop a broad hint about it. Tell him I think it would be worth his while, and I hope to see him here for the dinner on Friday."

Betty nodded and inserted a letter head into the typewriter. She was MWA's only paid employee, a pert little brunette who kept the office running, handling the extensive library, correspondence with members, and a thousand other chores.

The office itself was located on the second floor of a building just off Times Square. It was anything but fancy, with bookshelves lining two of its walls, filled to overflowing with mystery novels, mostly by members. The front window looked down on 48th Street, and if one stood close enough he could see the comings and goings at the restaurant downstairs. Toward the back of the long, somewhat narrow room that served as MWA's headquarters, there was a storage area and a sink—and it was this part of the office which served as the bar during the group's monthly cocktail parties.

Now, with only the two of them in the office, it seemed spacious and relaxing. When fifty or seventy-five members crowded in for the cocktail parties or monthly meetings, it took on more of the air of a Paris bistro or a rush-hour subway car.

"The awards are all set, I suppose?" Barney asked her.

"All set."

"The statuettes are up from Virginia?"

"Yes."

The ceramic Edgar and Raven statuettes given as awards were produced by Virginia Davis in Lynchburg, from the original designs by Peter Williams.

"Let's see. What else? The programs—the MWA Annual—all printed and delivered?"

"Right."

He grunted and lit a cigarette. That seemed to cover it all. Somebody else, another committee, was handling the dinner arrangements at the Biltmore.

"Who's the Reader of the Year Award going to, again?"

"Craigthorn. Ross Craigthorn. You know, Barney! He's on television every night."

"I watch Cronkite," Barney said.

He shuffled through the mail and glanced at some of the return addresses, looking for familiar names.

"Well . . . I guess maybe I'll hop over to Harry's and talk to him."

"Will you be back in case anybody's looking for you?"

"Probably. Late this afternoon."

People were always looking for Barney Hamet, especially this week, with the Awards Dinner coming up. Barney was executive vice president of MWA, and in the loose-knit structure of the organization, he held perhaps the most important post.

The president this year was a recluse mystery writer from the wilds of Montana who rarely came down to civilization. He had accepted the honor and sent a brief telegram acknowledging it, but Barney doubted if he would ever venture into New York City, even for the annual dinner of the organization. Most years, the presidency went to a name writer in the field, someone the public knew and admired—someone who neither wanted the work involved, nor was capable of handling the many small organizational details. All that fell in the lap of the executive vice president.

Barney Hamet's writing was tending to suffer with his job as exec VP, but it was good to be between things occasionally. He'd once told his ex-wife that he was always between things, and she didn't appreciate the remark. Barney had started writing right out of high school, contributing stories and even an occasional poem to the various little magazines around New York, graduating finally to a quite spectacular short mystery story, which was purchased for a

16

thousand dollars by one of the leading women's magazines.

Such a sale at the age of nineteen would have been remarkable in itself, but what made it all the more remarkable was the fact that the solution to Barney's mystery hinged on a scientifically impossible fact. The letters poured in to the editor. A lengthy explanation and apology was published two months later, and Barney Hamet's writing career was almost over before it had begun. He wrote a couple of other things, but of course the editor was wary of them. They came back by return mail and Barney settled into the dull business of collecting rejection slips.

If the writing languished, the rest of his life did not. He entered college, stayed there a year, then left and took a job with a small private detective agency up in Westchester. It was not at all the type of thing he'd expected or the type of life he wanted to lead for the next forty years. Dull divorce cases, mainly. Not even the predawn breaking into bedrooms that he used to read about and imagine. The most excitement came when he was assigned to a shopping center supermarket to check on shoplifters. He'd caught one hefty woman carrying out two heads of cabbage in her bosom, and felt that the job had been worth it after all.

Five years later, though, he gave it up and went back to writing. The experience of being a private detective somehow glamorized him beyond all expectations. His first story sold immediately to one of the mystery magazines, and then his second, and his third. Another went to a men's magazine. The money began to roll in, and a paperbound publisher even asked him for a novel.

It was about this time that he realized one of the big things going for him was his name. Although he spelled it H-A-M-E-T, he pronounced it exactly like Dashiell Hammett's. And of course Dashiell Hammett had also been a private detective back in his early days. One editor started billing him as the second Hammett, but there was really no comparison. Despite the private-eye background, Barney did not write the tough type of realism at which Hammett had excelled. His stories were gimmicky little studies in paradox. Closer, some critics thought, to Chesterton than to Chandler or Hammett.

If his writing never hit the really big time in the field, he was now, at the age of thirty, in an enviable position in the profession. His peers had selected him as their executive vice president. He appeared regularly on New York television, on all-night radio shows, and on panel discussions. He spoke occasionally to a writing class at Columbia University and had even been invited to teach a course at Fordham next season.

But all that was in the past. Now his main concern was the MWA dinner. He paused on his way to the door and asked Betty, "You're going to type up the final seating arrangement with those last-minute corrections?"

She tossed her dark hair and nodded. "Of course. Don't worry so much."

"We can probably get you some help if you need it for this week—a girl from one of the temporary services. Or somebody's wife."

"I may need a typist, come about Wednesday. We'll see."

"Okay, Betty," he said. "I'm really going over to see Harry now."

But again he didn't quite make it to the door. Someone was coming up the narrow staircase, light footed and sure of herself. He knew, without even opening the door, that it was someone seeking him. It was that sort of a week.

The girl who appeared in the doorway, almost bumping into him before she saw him, was tall and slender, with blonde hair and wild blue eyes. She wore a neat looking blue-skirted suit, and carried a purse large enough to have concealed anything from a gun to a notebook. As it turned out, it concealed the latter, and she produced it almost at once.

"I'm Susan Veldt," she said.

"Should I know you?"

"Susan Veldt, staff writer for *Manhattan* magazine. Didn't they call you?"

He turned back into the office. "Betty, did anyone call from *Manhattan*?"

"Now while I was here."

"Well," the girl said, "that just shows what sort of effi-

18

ciency there is in the world these days. Anyway, I'm Susan Veldt, as I said, and I've come to interview Barney Hamet. About the dinner, you know."

"I'm Barney Hamet."

"Good!"

"The interview's for *Manhattan*?" It seemed like a great publicity break.

"Yes. I'm going to be there. I sent in my twelve-fifty for a ticket."

"All right," Barney said, indicating a seat. "Let's talk it over. Always glad of the publicity—and you've got a good little magazine there. What is it you want to know?"

She sat opposite him, pencil out, very calm and sure of herself. "Well now, let's see . . . I guess first I'd better tell you what I'm doing. We're running a series of six articles in *Manhattan*—perhaps you've seen some of them—on the various awards that are presented in New York every spring. We've covered the Grammys already, and the National Book Awards, and the Tonys. I guess you're next, before the Pulitzers and the Emmys." She pointed toward the bookshelf where an Edgar and a Raven stood side by side. "Is that one of the Edgars over there?"

"That's right," he said. "Bust of Edgar Allan Poe—ceramic."

"How tall is it?"

"About nine and a half inches. Call it ten, if you want. They're made for us by a gal down in Virginia, then shipped up here. A man named Peter Williams designed both the Edgar and the Raven you see next to it. The Edgar is a writing award, given each year for the best novel, best first novel, best short story, television show, screenplay—that sort of thing. The Raven is given less frequently, although we usually award one or two each year. It's what might be called a non-writing honor, although it often goes to our members—people who have helped us out in one way or another."

"I understand there's also a readers' award that's given."

"Yes. That's correct. We've had some famous people named Reader of the Year. Eleanor Roosevelt won it one year—and a few other big names. Joey Adams, I believe, was one of the winners, too. This year, of course, you probably know it's Ross Craigthorn."

Betty snorted and shot him a glance. He'd been asking her about the award not ten minutes earlier.

"The actual announcement won't be made till the dinner itself, of course, but we don't keep it as secret as the writing awards. I think one or two of the gossip columnists have even carried it already."

"Craigthorn is an important person to have at your dinner."

Barney smiled at her. "We like to think it's an important dinner."

"It's at the Biltmore?"

"Right. The bar opens at six. Dinner at seven-thirty. Awards at nine. We've had it there for the last few years—ever since they tore down the Astor. Way back in the forties and fifties we used to put on a little show that went with it. Members like Clayton Rawson and John Dickson Carr and Joe Commings worked for months on it. The thing was so much work, in fact, that we finally had to abandon it."

Susan Veldt bit at her pencil. "Tell me something about yourself. You're the executive vice president—right?"

"Right."

"I've never read any of your stories."

"That's not surprising. A lot of people haven't."

"What did you do before you started to write?"

"Should I tell you I was a private detective?"

"Tell me if it's true."

"It is true. I was a private detective up in Westchester. I caught a few shoplifters, caused a few divorces. Nothing as glamorous as in the books."

"You sound bitter."

"I sound realistic."

"Listen, Barney—is it all right if I call you Barney?"

"Sure."

"Listen, Barney—I'm supposed to be the tough one. I'm supposed to be able to handle any of you guys I talk to. You're something new to me, though."

"I try to be something new to all the girls," he said.

20

"Married?" she asked.

"Divorced."

"Was that one of the divorces you arranged while you were a private eye?"

"No. She arranged it."

"Is she in the city?"

"She's in Mexico, or Africa, or maybe even Australia, for all I know. She was always a great traveler. But the story needn't concern me. It's about the Awards Dinner, isn't it?"

"Who's the president of your organization this year?"

Barney gestured toward one of the shelves. "See those twenty volumes? They're all his. He lives in Montana, in a little cabin up in the woods. He writes a book a year, and nobody ever sees him. For all I know it's probably Ambrose Bierce, come back from the dead."

"So you're going to be the top MWA executive at the dinner. You'll be running the show."

"I'll be acting as MC, introducing the speakers—that sort of thing. I wouldn't really say I'll be running the show. I've got a lot of big people coming. Rex Stout usually comes. Perhaps Charlotte Armstrong from California. Max Winters, I think, will be there—Kenneth Millar (his pen name's Ross Macdonald) and his wife, Margaret. We get maybe three hundred people for these things. Editors too, of course. All the mystery editors. Ernie Hutter from Hitchcock's magazine is coming up from Florida, and we hope that Fred Dannay—he's half of Ellery Queen—will be able to make it. Clayton Rawson, of course, Hans Stefan Santesson—and some editors outside the mystery field, from magazines like *Argosy*. Bruce Cassidy on *Argosy*, of course, is one of our members. Who else? Oh . . . Lee Wright from Random House—lots of book editors."

"And I'll be representing *Manhattan* magazine. I feel quite honored."

Barney lit another cigarette. "Who's your editor over there these days?"

"Arthur Rowe. Do you know him?"

"Never met him, but I've heard the name. He's got a good reputation in the field. I wish he published fiction. I'd send him a few short stories."

21

"No fiction for us. Just fact."

"I've read a couple of things in *Manhattan*. Sometimes it reads more like fiction."

"I hope you don't mean my things."

"Susan Veldt . . . how's that spelled? V-E-L-D-T?"

"Yes, that's right—like the grassy plains of South Africa. Open, and a bit dangerous."

"Oh? Can't really say that I remember you. They should put your picture with the articles, and then I'd remember them for sure."

"I guess that's meant to be a compliment."

"I guess," he said.

"Would it be possible for me to get over to the Biltmore and see the room before the dinner?"

"Perhaps. I'm going to call on somebody about the dinner right now. You can tag along, if you want. If you won't find it too boring."

"I never find it boring to be in the company of a handsome man."

"Now it's my turn to thank you for the compliment."

"You're welcome."

He called over to Betty, ignoring her frown of exasperation. "I'll try to get back, or phone at least, late in the day. Then we'll see if there are any other last-minute problems. Get that letter off to Max, though. That's important."

Barney strolled over to Fifth Avenue with Susan Veldt and then down a few blocks to a nondescript office building with an airline ticket office on its ground floor. They took the elevator to the top, which wasn't very high as Fifth Avenue buildings to, and then down a narrow corridor beginning to show signs of age.

"I want you to meet Harry Fox," Barney told her. "He's very active in the organization, even though he's only an associate member. Does just about everything except write mysteries. He's on the planning committee for the dinner."

"Oh?" She glanced at the door before which they'd paused. "Harry Fox Enterprises? Sounds mysterious."

"Not really. A small-time theatrical agent. That sort of thing."

They knocked and entered. There was no secretary—only one large room filled with filing cabinets in a general state of disarray. The walls were hung with framed photographs, most of them showing a jovial, youngish man with his arms around one or another small-time night club comedian or Hollywood starlet.

Harry Fox himself, in the flesh, sat behind a desk in one corner of the uproar. He was middle-aged, almost completely bald and shorter by a head than Barney's six-foot-one. The photographs on the wall depicted a younger man, and it was obvious they had been taken a good decade earlier.

"Well, well!" Harry said, rising to meet then. "Always glad to see you, Barney, especially when you're accompanied by a beautiful young lady. Pull up some chairs and tell me what's on your mind."

Barney held a chair for Susan Veldt and then took one himself. "The beautiful young lady is a magazine writer, Harry. She's doing a piece on the MWA dinner. Susan Veldt, Harry Fox."

Harry gave a little bow and reached out his hand. "Pleased to meet you, Miss Veldt—V-E-L-D-T? . . . like in Africa?"

"That's right," she said, with a trace of a smile. "Like in Africa."

Harry grunted. "Well, anyway, it's good to have visitors today. It was sort of slow. I just sit here waiting for clients who never come."

"You're not a writer yourself?" Susan asked him.

"No such luck. Not at fiction, at least. I've done a couple of articles for some fan magazines, but there aren't even as many of those as in the science-fiction field. Fellow named Allen Hubin edits a good one—*The Armchair Detective*. People keep telling me I picked the wrong phase of writing for my hobby."

"But you know a lot about mysteries?" she asked.

Barney interrupted to explain. "Harry knows a lot about everything, especially the beginnings of the mystery story. He's pretty much of an expert on nineteenth-century stuff—Poe and the like."

23

"Poe?"

"Ask me something," Harry said, "so I can impress you with my brilliance."

"I guess I don't know what to ask," Susan replied, seeming for once at a loss for words.

"Well . . ." Harry leaned back in his chair, his mind wandering over the card file of facts behind his deep brown eyes. "How about the first detective story, 'The Murders in the Rue Morgue'?"

"What about it?"

"Ever wonder where he got the name of his detective—Dupin? It seems that Poe was a book reviewer for various publications, and he had just reviewed a book called *Conspicuous Living Characters of France*. Well, one of the conspicuous living characters was a French politician named Dupin. He was described as a person of antithetical qualities, a living encyclopedia and a believer in legal methods. That seemed to impress Poe enough so that he named his detective after the man—though of course they never met."

"I'm impressed," Susan Veldt assured him. "Even though I haven't read 'The Murders in the Rue Morgue' since high school. That was the one about the gorilla, wasn't it?"

Barney smiled. "Not really a gorilla—more of a ourangoutang, I believe. Give her another fact, Harry. I can see she's hard to impress today."

"Gladly, gladly. Always pleased to oblige. Do you remember those serials they used to have in our youth?" He squinted at her. "Guess you're too young to remember them. Anyway, back in the thirties and forties they had these serials and they'd show 'em in the movie houses on a Saturday afternoon and just about everyone of them would have a chapter ending where the wall of a room was gradually coming out to crush our hero."

Now it was Susan Veldt's turn to interrupt. "I know! 'The Pit and the Pendulum'! I remember that Poe story too."

"Fine! Fine! We're getting along famously. Now can you tell me who was the first writer to use a wall gimmick like that, with the room growing smaller and crushing the hero? Someone before Poe?"

24

"I can't imagine. Do they copyright ideas like that?"

"Well, the closing room came from a story called 'The Iron Shroud' by William Huntley. It appeared in the August 1830, issue of *Blackwood's Magazine*."

Susan held up her hands in mock surrender. "All right. You're a walking encyclopedia and I'm the first one to admit it. I guess I'd better do something on the dinner, though, and that's what I need the facts for."

"Anything I can tell you," Harry offered.

She thumbed through her notebook pages, reading. "The Edgars are named in honor of Edgar Allan Poe, and the Ravens, those ceramic black birds, are named for his most famous poem."

"Correct," Barney said. "I'll bet you didn't have that easy a time with the other awards. What about the Emmys and the Oscars and all those?"

Susan had done her homework well. She ticked them off on her fingers. "I didn't work on the Oscars, so I can't answer for that. I understand there are some contradictory explanations for the origin of the name. The Grammys, of course, are named after the gramophone. Tonys are a shortened version of the Antoinette Perry Awards, the original name for them. You know the Edgars yourself. Any other questions?"

"How about the Emmys—the television awards?"

"I don't do that story till next month, but I can answer it in advance if you'd like. The name Emmy comes from Immy. It's an engineering term, relating to the image orthocon, or in layman's language, a television camera tube."

Now it was Harry Fox's turn to be impressed. "This girl's a regular whiz, isn't she?"

Barney agreed. "Hope she's that much of a whiz when she's publicizing our dinner. You're not one of these sarcastic bitches, are you?"

"Please!" she said, pretending mild shock. "Do I look like one?"

"Looks can be deceiving. Harry, why don't you run over the lineup and tell her what's what?"

"Gladly," Fox said, clearing off a space on his desk where he could flip through the schedule of awards presentations.

"I don't want to get too specific about this, especially not about who won the awards and such, but we'll start out with a little opening speech, which, oddly enough, I'm going to give myself this year, just because there has to be someone to introduce Barney. Then Barney takes it from there, runs through the various awards. Before the actual writing awards we'll probably take a break and give our Reader of the Year Award to Ross Craigthorn. After that we get to the juvenile, short story, true crime, best first novel and best novel. That's about it. Each winner comes up, at least the ones that are present come up. They say a few words, take their award . . ."

"What about these scrolls Barney mentioned on the way over?" she asked.

"Well, we usually have several nominees in each category. Occasionally we only have one, but sometimes there are as many as six. Each nominee gets a scroll, whether they're an Edgar winner or not. The scrolls are hand-lettered by Douglas Waugh. We have ushers stationed around the room to deliver the scrolls personally to the tables, so it's not necessary for the nominees to come up to the podium. After the scrolls are distributed, we read off the name of the winner and he comes up—or whoever is to accept the award comes up in his place. It runs quite smoothly."

"How long does it last?"

"Well, the dinner is timed pretty carefully to be over about nine. The awards take a bit over an hour, depending on how long-winded our principal speaker is. Generally, they talk for fifteen, twenty minutes or so. Since the reader's award usually goes to an entertainment figure of some sort, they have a few witty sayings—things like that. It's hard to tell how long Craigthorn will talk. He's no comedian, but he might get into personal reminiscences or something like that."

"Would it be possible for me to see the dining room before the dinner?"

Harry Fox glanced at his watch. "Actually, I was going to go over there and talk to the assistant manager about arrangements. You're welcome to come over with me if you want. Barney, I think you should be there, too, since you're the exec VP. I'm only an associate member and I hardly feel free to spend the organization's money myself."

"Okay," Barney said. "Let's go"

"Were all these people your clients? I didn't know you had any television personalities." He'd walked over to the wall and was glancing at the pictures.

Harry Fox grunted. "Some of them are friends. Some were pictures taken in barrooms. I put 'em up on the wall to fill the space. It looks impressive. I wish a few of them were my clients. Then maybe I could afford a better office than this." He shepherded them out and locked the door. They went down in the elevator, aware of its creakings and groanings, and out finally onto a sundrenched Fifth Avenue that was as crowded as always.

Chapter Four

SUSAN VELDT

The next day was rainy in Manhattan—one of those heavy April rains that seems to pick up the Atlantic Ocean and throw it down with force on the island.

Susan came out of her apartment opposite Central Park and decided it would be foolish to spend twenty minutes waiting in the rain for one of the infrequent buses on the Avenue. If she'd been down further, below 59th, she'd have had a fighting chance, but up here what buses there were seemed to delight in disappearing with the first rain—like New York taxis, only larger. She was lucky in grabbing a cab, though, and before long she had settled back somewhat damply onto the smelly leather seat. When she'd managed to compose herself a bit and wipe the dampness from her face, she opened her flowery attaché case to peer at the notes she'd made of yesterday's activities.

Outside, the rain beat against the taxi windows, each drop flattening and running down in an endless stream that blurred all vision and disjointed any view of reality. She might have been a person alone at that hour of the morning, except for the humming cab driver, whose presence to her was only the smooth hair on the back of his neck. He was a man, and the first man she'd seen that morning close up, but he might only have been a machine, an extension of the internal combustion engine carrying her to her destination.

The day before had gone well, and she found herself actually liking Barney Hamet in a strange sort of nonromantic way. He was all bulges and bristles in the right places, and gave the impression of being the sort that got a job done.

After the tour of the Biltmore with him and that other strange man, Harry Fox, she'd gone last night to the Eighth Street Bookstore, where she occasionally found titles difficult to locate elsewhere. She'd pondered over their paperbound mystery section, stuck way up on the highest level, and found there—right ahead of Dashiell Hammett—two of the novels that Barney Hamet had turned out.

She read one late that night, snuggled deep within the blankets of her bed, trying to imagine herself as the heroine, and Barney as the hero. But it didn't work out, because the hero, a slick sort of police detective, was exactly the type she imagined most of the men in the world to be, and if this was Barney, she wanted no part of him.

She had to admit, though, that the book had a certain pace, not bad for its sort, and she'd stuffed it into her attaché case, along with the unread one, thinking that they might provide useful research in the later stages of the article.

When she reached the office, she found the tiny reception room cluttered with umbrellas opened to dry like a field of mushrooms and damp, dripping secretaries struggling with spoiled hairdos. She walked through their midst, imperious as always, paying little attention to these office nobodies, aligning herself with the men, who typed and smoked and typed some more in the little cubbyhole offices clustered around Arthur Rowe's sanctum.

When on a long story, she had a habit of typing up a rough draft and leaving it in Rowe's *In* box for further discussion before she attempted the completed article. She did this now, typing fast with little thought to style, getting down the facts about Hamet and the interesting visit to Harry Fox's cluttered office. She went into the arrangements at the Biltmore a little, but not too much, preferring to save them for a description of the dinner itself.

Rowe was out—off somewhere in ponderous pursuit of a new Broadway opening, and she left the rough draft in his box.

After lunch she phoned Barney Hamet at MWA headquarters. "Remember me? Susan Veldt, from yesterday?"

"How could I forget?"

"I was wondering how things were coming."

"Pretty well. Everything usually falls into place at the last minute."

"You said something yesterday about craft sessions— some panel discussions of editors and such that precede the dinner itself . . ."

"Yes. Those will be Thursday night and Friday afternoon. We have some people flying in for them. Editors are such."

"Would it be worth my while to come over for them?"

"I don't think so. They're not really a part of the actual awards event, and that's what you're interested in, isn't it?"

"I suppose so," she said.

There was a pause, and she waited for him to say something. But when it came, she was disappointed. "Look, I've got to rush now. A million things to take care of. Phone me later in the week, and we'll make arrangements for you. You said you bought a ticket. Is one enough? Your editor doesn't want to come, does he?"

She tried to picture Arthur Rowe among the denizens of the mystery-writing world. "No." She chuckled a bit. "I don't think so."

She put down the phone and stared out the window at the rain, feeling oddly empty, disjointed. The conversation had been unsatisfactory, but then, what had she expected? She was a gal who hated most men, and there was no reason for her to feel otherwise about Barney Hamet. Still . . . the thing bothered her.

Chapter Five

BARNEY HAMET

On Thursday morning, quite early, Barney drove out to Kennedy Airport through a disjointed web of Long Island highways shuttling office workers to their rush-hour jobs. It was a bad time to travel anywhere in New York, but he couldn't help that. Max Winters had agreed to come, and was flying in from the Coast. This year, with the best-novel Edgar in the offing, Max was the most important guest the dinner would have, with the possible exception of Ross Craigthorn. Barney felt, through friendship and duty, that it was his place to meet Max at the airport rather than leave the fellow at the mercy of New York cab drivers.

He arrived early and paced the floor of the airline waiting room until at last Max came through the swinging doors, all bushy beard and scraggly hair, looking as if he'd flown from the coast in a little one-seater plane with an open cockpit.

"Barney, my boy! Barney—you old son of a bitch! I'm glad to see you! What's been going on back east? Have I missed much? Are you gonna give me an award, after all these years?"

Barney smiled slightly as he took the great paw of a hand that Max offered. "It's always good to see you, Max. I should be asking you how things are on the Coast. That's where all the action is these days. Do you realize how many nominees we're getting from out that way?"

"We're vital, Barney! Vital! I was up at Berkeley the other day. Wild things going on there!"

"Demonstrations?"

"No . . . not demonstrations. Just thinking. We live in such a massive bone-busting time, I just wish we could get some of this energy on paper! You know, the mysteries we're writing today, if we're ever going to preserve the unity of the form, have got to appeal to the young. It's all very fine to write 'em for the nice, middle-aged ladies who go down to the library and pick up a stack of them at one time for reading in bed, but we've got to reach the kids, and how are we gonna do that?"

"Great speech, Max! Save it for the craft session tonight. I'll put you on first."

"Still the same old Barney, aren't you? The tough private-eye image. I thought maybe being exec VP had mellowed you a bit."

"Max, nothing's ever going to mellow me."

"Find a good woman, and she'll do it."

"Good women are a dime a dozen around New York. I ran into one on the way home last night. She was standing under a lamp post and gazing out at the world. Looked for all the world like a philosopher."

"Maybe she was," Max said. "Maybe those are the best kind."

"When are you going to shave off that damn beard, anyway?"

"It's my image, Barney! My image! I got it on the backs of the book jackets and, you know, they have me on these panel discussion shows out on the Coast—and everybody expects me to have a beard. Without the beard, what am I? A weak-chinned middle-aged man. Beards are in, Barney. I might even write an article about it—about the period in our government's history, back around Lincoln and Grant's time, when even the presidents all had beards. It was a vital time. A lot more vital than our founding fathers with their smooth-shaven faces and powdered wigs."

"I don't think there was anything too vital about Grant,

except the way he drank whiskey."

"Nevertheless," Max started, then chuckled and slapped Barney on the back. "You got your car outside?"

"Yeah, I'm going to give you a real treat, drive you in to New York myself, right to the hotel."

"Where you got me staying? One of those new places with all chrome and sealed windows you can't even open?"

"That's right. Just the place for you, Max."

They chatted on the ride in, and Barney found that his liking for Max had not dimmed in the year or so since he'd seen him last. Max was a good friend, a good writer, a good talker. The business needed more men like Max Winters.

He saw him to his room, explained about the craft session that evening and then left him to make his way around the city as best he could. It was Thursday, the day before the dinner, and Barney had other chores.

One of them was to telephone Ross Craigthorn at Amalgamated Broadcasting. He called from a phone in the hotel lobby. It took him a while to get through to the man, and when he did, the voice on the other end was just a little bit testy. "I'm preparing the script for my afternoon taping," Craigthorn said. "I don't have too long."

"This is Barney Hamet."

"I know. The secretary told me who you were."

"I'm helping with arrangements for tomorrow night's dinner, and I just want to make sure you're clear on everything. The bar opens at six, but perhaps you won't want to mingle with the people too much before dinner. We would like you to be there by seven-thirty, though."

"I'll come around seven or so."

"Will your wife be joining you?"

"No. My wife is . . ." The pause lengthened before he finished the sentence. "Away."

"All right," Barney said. "I'll see you tomorrow night, then."

He hung up the telephone and walked briskly through the hotel lobby to the street. There were other people to be contacted, but he'd have to wait for most of them until the dinner itself. In the time before they were seated, he could chat with a few people.

He dropped by the office to see how Betty Rafferty was handling the last-minute arrangements. "You have the seating list all mimeographed?"

"Final form, Barney. All set."

"Good." He picked up the phone and dialed a New Jersey number he knew by heart—Mike Avallone's home telephone number. He wanted to check and make sure Mike would be handling the lights, directing the spotlight to follow the winners as they went to the rostrum for their awards.

After a lengthy and friendly chat with Mike, he phoned James Reach, a past president of the organization, and checked some arrangements with him. Since the current president was still off in Montana somewhere, Barney felt they should introduce a few past presidents—anyone who was going to be there. The list was slim, since many of them were out of town, and Tony Boucher had died since the last dinner—but with Reach, Larry Blochman, Rex Stout and one or two others, he felt he could get together a decent enough program.

Finally, with no time to spare, he was off to the craft session.

Chapter Six

VICTOR JONES

It had not been difficult to gain admittance to the nineteenth floor of the Biltmore Hotel, where the ballroom that Thursday evening was housing the final stages of a hardware convention. The layout of the place lent itself well to an intruder. Victor Jones had simply strolled in, mistaken by the waiters for a tardy guest, and by the guests for some management functionary checking on the proceedings.

He knew a visit the following day was in order because the rostrum might be in a different position—but still, this gave him an overall view of the ballroom, and it was necessary before he could proceed with the final phase of his plan.

He'd called Ross Craigthorn one more time, but the conversation had been unsatisfactory to both of them. He knew now there was no hope, and that he would have to act.

Later that night, he spent some time in a little home workshop he sometimes used. He had a number of things there, but the ones that most interested him at the moment were the transmitting and receiving units from a cheap citizens'-band radio outfit, a piece of narrow metal tubing, and some .38 caliber bullets. He had a quantity of copper wire, also—and a tiny drill which he used along with a soldering iron to carefully attach the wire to the cartridge case of the bullet.

The wire had to go through a minute aperture in the back of the cartridge case—then almost, but not quite, connect with another wire. There had to be a bridge there—a bridge just the right distance for a spark to jump. That spark would set off the powder in the cartridge and propel the bullet forward.

He tried it three times before it worked to his satisfaction. Then he packed up the gear very carefully in a small suitcase, ready for tomorrow night's dinner.

He turned on the television news at one A.M. on Amalgamated. Ross Craigthorn was long gone from the studio, but they had a taped replay of an earlier interview of his. Victor Jones sat and looked at the man he was going to kill, remembering those days long ago when they'd sworn that nothing could ever come between them. Something had, of course. Life had. Everyone changes. For the better, or for the worse.

He couldn't really decide whether Ross Craigthorn was a better or a worse man than when they'd both been young. But whatever the change, it was a danger now to Victor Jones.

Chapter Seven

BARNEY HAMET

Friday was sunny—warm and sunny—a good day for the rest of the visitors who would be coming from out of town. The weather would not interfere with the dinner's attendance, and that made Barney happy.

He was up early, because there were people to meet, things to do. He'd had a few drinks with Max Winters the previous evening, after the craft session, and although they'd parted before midnight, Barney still felt sleepy. The bed in his furnished uptown apartment was not the most comfortable in the world.

Barney went first to the Fifth Avenue office of Harry Fox. Surprisingly, for the early hour, Harry was not alone. He was using his publicity ability on a sleepy gentleman whom Barney knew slightly. Harry introduced them again, just for the record. "Barney, you know Skinny Simon, don't you?"

Barney had met Skinny Simon once or twice before, but knew the man mainly by his reputation, as did almost everyone else in New York. Skinny Simon was not really skinny; he was tall, with a fairly medium build, and whether his name truly was Simon perhaps only his mother could say. But he had a reputation. He was one of the "in" people these days. He conducted an all-night radio show that made his name a household word within listening distance of New York. Once a week he also did an hour-long television show, but it was with the radio show that he had really achieved the sort of instant fame possible only in the media of modern American entertainment.

He actually was following in the footsteps of a number of other personalities—people like Long John Nebel—who attracted the weird, the controversial, the interesting, and managed to keep a good many New Yorkers awake from twelve to five every morning. The shows had been going on in Manhattan and Los Angeles for years, and seemed as popular and as exasperating as ever. Some seasons back, one had been conducted by a magician named "The Amazing Randy," and others came and went on the airways almost as fast as the seasons changed.

Skinny Simon had survived longer than most. He wore a fashionable brown beard and close-cropped hair that gave him an air of timelessness. He might have been thirty, or forty, or even older. No one exactly knew. Nor did they know where he had come from. They only knew where he was going—to the top. He had tended, in recent seasons, to be more and more controversial, attracting political figures, small-time fascists, black nationalists and the like.

But he still tended, occasionally, to return to his first love, the saucer people—that odd cult of New Yorkers who met regularly to discuss the latest sightings, to plan for meetings with visitors from outer space. There were more than a handful of people walking the streets of Manhattan who claimed to be from other planets, and Skinny Simon provided them with a forum. Barney had listened in awed admiration all one night while Skinny interviewed a girl who claimed to be from Mars—claimed to have taken the body of a suicidal beauty queen who'd slashed her wrists in a Harlem hotel back in 1957.

They got a little kidding from Skinny, but generally they accepted it. It was exposure to them, and exposure was what they usually wanted. Skinny usually let the nuts and kooks have their say. It was only with the political and racial figures that he was beginning of late to unleash his sharp-edged stiletto.

"Glad to meet you again, Skinny," Barney said, extending his hand. The bearded man accepted it.

"Just who I wanted to see. You know, I was up here talking to Harry about a show I want to do over the weekend. I know I should have planned it sooner, but a panel I had planned for Sunday night sort of fizzled out. They were a group of ghost hunters, and I hear they've gone up to Maine after a ghost whale somebody saw! Would you believe a ghost *whale*? Anyway, I'm looking for something to replace them and it occurred to me that with your dinner tonight, you probably have a lot of mystery writers in town. I could get together a show . . ."

Barney interrupted. "Sunday night—it's a little bad. A lot of the people will be leaving Sunday morning for home. You see, the dinner's tonight and we have a cocktail party at MWA headquarters tomorrow night, but after that the festivities are pretty much over. You might get a few people staying till Monday, but nobody who has to get back to a regular job."

"You mean you mystery writers *work*?"

Harry Fox chuckled, and Barney answered, "Some of us do and some of us don't. The really successful ones don't." He paused and corrected himself. "No . . . that's not always true either. It's a funny thing. You'll get a guy you never heard of who's turning out sex books once a month and he probably can make enough to live on doing just that—holed up in a little apartment over in Queens somewhere. On the other hand, you get a fairly successful mystery novelist who publishes no more than one book a year, and doesn't write short stories, and maybe it's tough for him to make a living on just that. So he has to do something else. Maybe he even has to prostitute his talents in advertising or public relations."

Skinny Simon smirked. "Or pimp for a few of his girlfriends, huh? Anyway, Barney, I still think it's a good idea if we can swing it. I was talking to Harry here, and he's agreed to come on the program. I'd like to get five writers in all. One or two big names—maybe Rex Stout or half of Ellery Queen."

Barney raised a hand. "Those people would be pretty

tough to get for an all-night show. They don't need the publicity, and those things are sort of wearing after the first few hours."

"You could try, couldn't you, Barney? Tell them it's for the good of the organization, all that stuff."

"I could try," Barney agreed.

Skinny took out a little pocket notebook covered in tan morocco leather and began jotting down names. "All right, I've got Harry Fox for sure. Then let's figure a big name like Stout or Queen. Who else is around?"

"Mike Avallone, perhaps," Barney suggested. "Jean Potts? She's a nice gal. Give you a little feminine interest, if she'll go for it."

"How about this year's award winners? That would be timely."

Barney thought of Max Winters. "Well, it's a possibility. I don't want to mention any names yet, but I can talk to them at the dinner tonight and see if they'd be interested."

"See what you can do," Skinny said.

"You want five?"

"I'd settle for four. I'd like five. It would be Sunday night. The show starts at midnight—runs till five in the morning. We take a break, have a little food in the middle. See what you can do, huh?"

They shook hands again and Skinny Simon departed, with a wave to Harry.

"He's not a bad guy," Fox said, when they were alone. "Comes on pretty strong, but he's certainly made a name for himself around town. Ever watch him on TV?"

Barney shook his head. "I'm usually out Friday nights. I catch his radio show a couple nights a week, though. The first hour, at least. If it's interesting I'll maybe keep it on. Generally I doze off. You can just go so far with these mind readers and space travelers and general nuts."

"Are mystery writers general nuts?"

Barney chuckled. "Of course not. But look, they need an expert like you on that show—to keep us all in line. You could rattle off some history and really impress the listeners."

"I'll try," Harry said. "But by Sunday night I'll probably

40

be so exhausted I won't be able to keep awake."

"Whose table are you sitting at tonight, Harry?"

"Golly, I don't know. I always like to get close to Betty Rafferty, but she'll probably be up on the podium."

Barney nodded. Betty was a fairly good-looking gal and added a bit of glamour to the proceedings. "I'll check the list when I get back to the office and see where they put you."

He was just leaving when Harry came up with a thought. "You know—for Skinny's radio show, why don't we get an agent or an editor, or somebody like that? We shouldn't confine it just to authors."

"Not a bad idea. I'll give it some thought."

It was a busy day for Barney, and he called in to MWA headquarters to see how things were going there. Betty told him that most of the out-of-town members had arrived now and a few had drifted down to the Biltmore for the craft session. Barney remembered it was to be a discussion of agents and editors, and decided to go down himself in hopes of rounding up one or two for Skinny Simon's show.

The walk was only a few blocks and in the sunny April weather he didn't mind it a bit. Cabs passed him by, their lights glowing, and he wondered where they all were at rush hour, or after the theatre, or on a rainy day. It was only the sunny weather that brought them out, like dandelions at the first hint of spring.

The craft session was just breaking up as he got there. He stood in the back for a few minutes, listening to the closing remarks by Ernie Hutter from *Alfred Hitchcock's Mystery Magazine*. Then he bought a drink for Clayton Rawson and stood at the bar downstairs talking to him until he spotted an agent he knew slightly, hurrying across the lobby.

"Dick!" he called out. "Dick, wait a minute. Can I talk to you?"

Dick McMullen was a friendly, unassuming sort of guy. He'd been connected with various literary agencies in his career—first with Scott Meredith and later with Samuel French. But now he was in business for himself, operating

41

out of his apartment in Greenwich Village. He didn't have any big-name writers yet, but he did manage to keep a few lesser lights happy. Barney knew he sometimes placed things for Max Winters and he used that as an opening wedge. "Dick, did you handle Max's last novel?"

"No, not that one, Barney. He placed that direct. I'm trying to get him tied down, though. I think he's a good writer and I think I can really do something for him. Since you're asking me, I would take a wild guess that he's going to be the Edgar winner tonight."

Barney smiled. "Maybe, maybe. Look, Dick, you're a nice talkative guy. How'd you like to go on an all-night radio show Sunday night?"

Dick McMullen frowned, adding more creases to his already wrinkled forehead. He was still in his late thirties, but his face was weathered, as if he had stood in the bow of a ship during a tropical storm. Maybe it was just being around New York all your life. Maybe that gave you the look. Barney didn't know.

"What about it? Interested?"

McMullen kept on frowning. "Sunday night. All night? God—that's a long stretch! What is it? Long Jon's show?"

"Skinny Simon's. Just as many listeners. And easier to find on the dial. What do you think?"

"Who else is going to be there?"

"Harry Fox for sure. I just might ask Max, if he's still going to be around then."

"Get Max and I'll go on. How's that for a deal?"

"You're really trying to pin him down, aren't you?"

"I need writers, Barney! What good's an agent without writers? You know who I've got now? I've got a young college kid who writes short stories like crazy—sells 'em to the mystery magazines, and gets maybe a hundred or two every couple of months, and out of that I get my ten percent. He thinks I'm doing a great job for him, and I probably am, but what do I make off of it? Ten or twenty bucks a month! With that I can't even pay the rent on the apartment. I need novelists. At least if they get two thousand a crack, I get a couple of hundred out of it. And with foreign sales, a lot more. A novelist has a better chance of hitting the TV markets, too—and the movies, of course. That's where the big money is these days."

"Okay, Dick. Let me see what I can do with Max. I'll let you know at the dinner tonight. You're going to be there, aren't you?"

"Sure! Wouldn't miss it. I can take it off my income tax."

Barney patted him on the shoulder and moved off, glad that it had gone so well. They'd talked like old friends, even though they had nothing really in common. Agents had stopped trying to sell Barney, and sometimes he felt a little bad about it, but then he didn't write that much any more. He was an organizer, a worker. He helped plan the dinners and monthly meetings, kept MWA's books in order, kidded with Betty at the office, saw to it that things ran well—but the writing had slowed to a trickle in recent months. Though he still received occasional royalty checks, soon he knew he'd have to find a job like everyone else, if only to keep up the alimony payments to his ex-wife.

Barney was on the nineteenth floor of the Biltmore at exactly six-thirty to greet the first arrivals. Betty Rafferty and a couple of the other girls were working the desk, checking invitations, although an army of gate crashers could have gotten in if they'd had a mind to.

Barney moved out to the elevator, shook hands with James Reach and his wife, Alice, as they got off. He kept busy checking over the stack of mimeographed table seatings. There were to be 303 people at the dinner this year—a good crowd. They'd had more some years, but less in others. Over three hundred was a good crowd.

Mike Kingsley, a former executive vice president, was the next arrival. He had Barney's stocky build and carried himself well. He'd once practiced law, and now he was an insurance company executive. Barney left him chatting with Norma Shier, a former secretary of the group, and moved on.

He saw Rex Stout get off the elevator, and hurried to meet him. Rex carried himself well and anyone seeing him might have guessed his age at sixty or sixty-five—certainly not at over eighty. There was someone else, too, a photographer from Associated Press. He'd come to get pictures of

43

the winners, which was always awkward because Barney didn't want any of the winners to know about it until the formal presentation at the dinner itself.

He glanced around for Max and finally spotted him over near the bar. The room containing the bar was big in itself, but it was only really an entranceway to the Grand Ballroom at the Biltmore. The place was gradually beginning to fill with people mingling in small groups, standing at the bar chatting, sitting at a few of the little tables scattered around the place.

Barney put a firm hand on Max's elbow and guided him away from a young girl in a miniskirt who was an obvious guest attending her first dinner. "Max, how about getting your picture taken? We've got an AP guy here. He wants some pictures of the nominees."

"Well . . . I don't know about that. I'm not a winner yet."

"Come on, Max. Come on."

He corralled Rex Stout next, then posed them in a group. The AP photographer insisted he get in the picture, too, since the president of MWA was not attending. They took a few pictures and then he went off.

Hans Stefan Santesson had just come in and Barney wanted to talk with him. Hans, who'd edited magazines and anthologies for a good many years, was an old friend. They'd seen a lot of the city together, and Barney remembered one night when Hans had taken him down to a Greek restaurant. They'd stayed until early morning, enjoying the pseudo-belly dancers and the authentic Greeks who frequented the place.

Someone gave him a sheet of lighting cues, and he went in search of Mike Avallone, finally finding him at the table near the entrance. "Mike . . . here are the lighting cues. You can handle it, can't you?"

"I've been doing it for years," Mike said. His wife was wearing a striking gown of white, with silver sequins, and Barney took his eyes off her only to notice someone else who had just gotten off the elevator.

A tall, long-haired blonde, vaguely familiar. Then he remembered—Susan Veldt, the magazine writer. How could he have forgotten? He excused himself from the Avallones and moved over to greet her.

"How are you tonight? Let me buy you a drink." He led her by the arm, an arm nicely bared to the shoulder, as they squeezed their way through to a position at the bar. He waved to Larry Blochman further down, and ordered two Scotch and waters. "I hope that's okay. I should have asked what you drank."

"I drink Scotch," she said. "I drink just about anything."

"Do you have your notebook?"

"Right here in the purse."

"What do you want to know? We've been giving these awards since 1945. It started out with just a few awards—motion picture—radio—first novel. We didn't start giving the best novel award till 1953. In '58 we started a foreign film award, but that's pretty much merged with the regular film award now. We've given critics' awards off and on. The short story award started in 1947, the same as fact crime. Since 1960 we've given a juvenile mystery award, and since 1951 we've had a television award. In 1954 we started giving an award for the best book jacket. Now, of course, we have that split up into soft-bound and hard-bound books. In '57 we started giving the grand master award, too, although we don't give it every year. There won't be one this year. Another award made fairly infrequently, is to the Mystery Reader of the Year. Dorothy Kilgallen got one in 1956 and Phyllis McGinley in 1959. We had a special award to Mrs. Eleanor Roosevelt in 1958. Richard Watts, Jr. got the Reader's Award in '66 and in '68 it was Joey Adams. We're giving one this year, as you know, to Ross Craigthorn."

"Is he here yet?"

"No—and I'm sort of wishing he'd show up."

"He has a TV show about this time, doesn't he?"

Barney glanced at his watch. It was not yet seven. "I suppose that's it. It's not far from Amalgamated Studios, though. He should be here any minute."

"Are any of these people editors?"

"Quite a few," Barney said, trying unobtrusively to point them out. "That man standing over there is Bruce Cassidy, a fiction editor of *Argosy*, and Larry Shaw, a paperback editor. Just about all of the book publishers are represented. I'll point out more of them to you later. That woman is Natalie MacMurdy. That's Herbert Brean, a novelist, who has quite a good job with *Life* magazine. Hilary Waugh, one of our directors. Harold Q. Masur. Gloria Armoury—a former executive secretary. Pauline Bloom, George Harmon Coxe."

"Is Ellery Queen here?"

"Manny Lee never gets down for these things. Fred Dannay usually does. We were hoping he'd be here tonight, but I haven't seen him as yet."

"How about John Dickson Carr?"

"He lives down in Carolina now. I was talking to him on the phone the other day. He didn't think he'd be able to make it. Of course we have quite a representation from the West Coast—Margaret Millar, and her husband, Ross Macdonald. They sometimes fly in." He paused to check the alphabetized seating list. "But I guess they're not coming this year."

"There's really a lot of work to something like this, isn't there?"

"There's a lot of work to it if you're the one who's doing the work." He moved over to say a few words to Lee Wells, and then greeted Robert Arthur as he came in. There were always so many people to meet, but he felt that was one of his duties as executive vice president. Ira Levin and his wife were there and he chatted briefly with them, then moved on to introduce Helen McCloy to Susan. For everyone, he had the same introduction, "Susan Veldt. She's with *Manhattan* magazine."

"Do you write mysteries?" someone would ask.

And Susan would give them her brightest smile. "My writing is something of a mystery at times."

It was about seven-fifteen when Ross Craigthorn entered with a woman he introduced as his secretary. He had the same stiff authoritative manner that people liked to watch on their television screens, and he was immediately recognized by the line of writers and editors along the bar. There was much shaking of hands. Someone who knew him asked about his wife, a question he ignored, and he went on to introduce his secretary again.

"Miss Sweeney . . . Miss Sweeney, Barney Hamet. This is Miss Sweeney, my secretary. No—my wife couldn't make it tonight. She's tied up . . . yet . . . Miss Sweeney is sort of filling in for her."

He mumbled something and indicated another man behind him. But apparently this was only an editor that he knew. Barney had seen the fellow around. His name was Frank Jesset and he edited a string of third-rate confession magazines. Somehow his connection with Ross Craigthorn seemed nebulous to say the least.

There was more stirring from the direction of the elevator and Skinny Simon came in, shuffling along with sagging shoulders. His beard attracted little attention here, where perhaps ten percent of the males wore them, but there was still something impressive in his presence. He made straight for Ross Craigthorn, obviously considering them to be brothers in the great fraternity of broadcasting. There was always something a little condescending about Skinny when he was with writers, as if the spoken word certainly carried more weight with people these days than the printed word. Perhaps he was right. Barney didn't think so himself, but he'd been wrong about other things in the past.

Craigthorn, for his part, had little to say to Skinny. He seemed embarrassed and at a loss for words. Skinny finally had to buy himself a drink when it became obvious that Craigthorn was gripping his glass with determination.

Finally Skinny drifted over and was introduced to Susan Veldt. They quickly fell into an animated conversation which seemed to involve the latest additions to the Central Park Zoo across from Susan's apartment.

"They're serving at seven-thirty," Betty Rafferty reminded Barney, slipping up behind him.

Barney nodded. He hadn't been aware that the time was passing so quickly. He walked around the bend in the hallway and surveyed the great reaches of the Biltmore ballroom. With 303 people at thirty-one tables, the room was filled to virtual capacity. The tables were round, generally accommodating nine or ten people, but there were instances where special arrangements had caused an increase to twelve chairs. The speakers' platform, with its podium, was on the left side of the room, about halfway along the far wall, a position from which most people could view it quite well.

The ballroom must have been about three stories high—and some twenty feet off the floor was a railed walk, running all the way around the room. It was from there that Mike and the lighting engineer would handle the spots.

Barney walked up to check the microphone. He was aware suddenly that Susan Veldt had followed him into the room and was standing, drink in hand, observing him. She stood with her legs slightly apart, tightening the shimmery fabric of her floor-length formal. It was an appealing pose to Barney, giving just a hint of tomboyishness within the confines of the gown.

"What are you doing now?" she asked.

"Always have to check the sound system. No sense waiting until the last minute." He tapped the microphone, a long narrow instrument that pivoted in any direction. It was very handy for the rostrum, because Barney could speak himself and then turn it for the few words of acceptance by the winner. He casually noticed the wires running down from it, paying them no further attention. "Testing. One-two-three." He left the power on and walked back down to Susan. "Everything seems in order," he said.

The waiters were already depositing dishes of fruit salad at each place. The time was seven-twenty.

At exactly seven-thirty the waiters began ringing their gongs, herding the guests like so many sheep toward the narrow entrance to the ballroom. It was surprisingly fast work. Though most people still clutched a drink, they seemed willing to move to the inner room.

Barney himself would be sitting at table number five, near the rostrum, where he could jump up as soon as the dinner was finished to begin the awards.

As he entered he stopped at table twenty-three to say a few words to Jeanne Bernkopf, the Dutton editor, and Lee Wright from Random House. Then he moved on, talking to Joan Kahn from Harper & Row, and one of her star authors, John Creasey, representing the British equivalent of MWA—the Crime Writers' Association. Finally he seated himself between Betty Rafferty and Susan Veldt at the front table. He waved to Jay Garon, the agent, who was sitting with Lois Cole from Walker & Co.

"You got me a seat right next to you," Susan said. "That was very thoughtful."

"I always save it for my girlfriends, and this year I don't have one," Barney told her.

"I suppose I should consider that another compliment."

"Publicity's good for us and you've got a good magazine and I have to treat you well." The words sounded a bit too harsh, and he was sorry for them almost at once.

The waiters moved with rapid precision, allowing only so much time for each course. Then, with a great clatter of movement, they descended on the tables, clearing off the old dishes and bringing on the new. The fruit was followed by vegetable soup and finally by the main course of chicken with rice. It was a standard dinner, and although they liked to give the courses fancy names in the awards program, it rarely varied too much. When feeding over three hundred people, there isn't a great deal of variety to the menu.

There was always a flurry of table-hopping during the meal itself, and this year was no exception. Max Winters came over and Barney remembered the radio program. "Max, Skinny Simon wants to do an all-night radio show Sunday night with a bunch of mystery writers and editors and such. Will you still be here then?"

Max pondered. "Yes. I was thinking of staying until Monday. But . . . I don't know about it."

"We've got Harry Fox already and I was talking to Dick McMullen, the agent. He thought he might come on."

"Oh?" Max seemed interested, but said no more. He moved on, to be replaced by Morris Hershman and Chris Steinbrunner. Morris turned down the radio show because he would be out of town on Sunday. Barney remembered that Chris had done a few all-night stints in the past on WOR, and asked him if he'd be interested, but Chris too was busy.

"All right," Barney said. "I'll find someone afterwards."

Max Winters came back. "I forgot to mention it, Barney, but I'm having a little party in my hotel room afterwards, if you can stop by."

"I'll do that," Barney said. "I want to talk to you some more about Skinny Simon's show. I think it would be good publicity for the organization."

Dinner continued through coffee and dessert—an ice-cream cake that was surprisingly good. Then, as Barney was about to mount the podium, he was surprised to see Max Winters deep in conversation with Harry Fox. After a moment, Harry went up to the microphone himself.

"Ladies and gentlemen," he began, "I think you all know me. I'm Harry Fox. I've been around for a good many years as an associate member of this organization. Only wish I could sell a story and become an active."

There was a ripple of laughter, and some applause. Harry was a popular fellow.

"I know it's usually the place of the executive vice president to conduct this affair, but before I turn the microphone over to him I have a little surprise. You all know Barney Hamet. You know how well he's served us as a director, as regional vice president, and now as executive vice president. I don't think anyone in recent years has done more for Mystery Writers of America than Barney Hamet. Like his almost namesake, Dashiell Hammett, he's been a private detective as well as a writer, and he knows the things he writes about, and he's damn good at writing about them. In recent years he's given so much time to the organization that he's been forced to neglect some of his own writing. I want you to know that we appreciate this and I want Barney to know it too. I've been chosen by MWA's board of directors, for some slightly strange reason, to make a special award this evening. Since Barney is going to be emceeing the rest of the program, we decided to make it at the beginning rather than at the end. So, Barney, in recognition of the many long hours you've given the organization, I'm more than a little proud to award you this MWA Raven as a token of our gratitude."

There was a round of applause through the ballroom and Barney, startled, at a loss for words, stepped forward to grasp the black and white porcelain statuette. It was a bit smaller than the Edgar and a bit more stylized, but it was a handsome bird, a long-beaked raven that sat sleepily on its perch, eyeing the assembled guests. Its tail feathers hung down over the white base, and on its front were the words "MWA Special Award." Barney grasped it tightly and stepped to the microphone, pivoting it a bit so he could speak directly into it.

"I certainly appreciate this honor. I know perhaps more than any of you what a real honor it is. I know the others in the organization who have won it. Herbert Brean won it just the other year for the fine work he has done. I hope I can continue to work for the group because I feel there's much that needs to be accomplished. As we said in those words written long ago, when MWA began, *Crime does not pay enough*! It's our job to see that it pays a little more, to lift the standards in the field, and the income for the authors in the field. I've tried to do what I can and I will continue to." He raised the Raven above his head, in a gesture of pride. "Thanks very much."

The applause rose again as Barney stepped back from the microphone. When it died, he came forward to begin the main part of the evening.

"And now, to start off, our award for the best television program of the past year."

Once begun the awards went quickly. First the nominees were read off—anywhere from two to six names—and waiters, recruited for the purpose, took the scrolls to the appropriate tables. Up above, the spotlight shifted now and then to pick up those who were winning. There were still a few people moving from table to table, although most of them had settled down. Barney saw a bearded man he didn't know near the back of the ballroom.

After the television award came the Edgar for the best mystery movie of the year. For these awards, there was usually someone from the New York office of the studio to pick up the Edgar. Best book jackets followed with two awards—one for hardcover and another for paperback. The

51

writing awards would come next—juvenile, short story, first novel, and novel. But before those last four, there was a necessary pause. The Reader's Award, given occasionally to some celebrity who was known to be an avid mystery reader, was to go this year to Ross Craigthorn. Barney had located his table earlier and now he signaled him to come up.

"Now, ladies and gentelmen, we are going to give our award for Reader of the Year. As you know, this award is usually in the form of a blunt instrument, or some other murderous weapon. We've given a number of things in the past. This year we have here," he leaned over to pick it up, "a large club, such as used by cavemen in the past. We don't promise that it is too authentic, but it might be of good use for knocking some reticent politicians over the head. So now, without further ado, I present this award to a man we all know, a man who interrupts our dinners every night with the news of the world and, just occasionally, with the news of the mystery world, Mr. Ross Craigthorn of Amalgamated Broadcasting."

Now the applause rose higher than it had during the entire evening. Craigthorn was a big name. People knew and respected him, and it was something of a coup to get him to the MWA dinner. He rose—tall, handsome, the dignified face and voice they all knew from the television screen.

"Ladies and gentlemen of the mystery world," he began, "I deem it a special honor to be here with you tonight. As you know, I have occasionally mentioned, at the close of my nightly show, a mystery or suspense yarn that particularly intrigued, baffled, and delighted me. I have done this without any sort of under-the-counter handout or publishers' urging. In fact, I have never even received a free lunch for my efforts!"

A ripple of laughter bounced across the room.

"I've done it because I like mysteries. I've liked mysteries all my life." He paused and tilted the microphone a bit, speaking directly into it. "I feel that they serve a purpose, perhaps a purpose beyond entertainment, in this world. I do not at all go along with those who fear that they are corrupting our youth. Certainly they are far less corrupting than some of the sex books that clutter our bookstores these days. I suppose, though, you might say they corrupted me in a very special way."

He paused and cleared his throat, looking around the room as if trying to pick out someone. At one of the upfront tables Skinny Simon stirred restlessly and drank from his water glass.

"I'm going to tell you something now that I've never told anyone before in my life. Something that is unknown to the television audience, although I hardly expect it will remain a secret after I reveal it here tonight. I'm going to tell you about two boys, or young men, if you will, alone in the world of some twenty-two years ago. You remember that time—it was soon after the war. A lot of people were mixed up. I was among them. We were both among them.

"It was my friend who got me interested in mystery reading, really. He was a great fan of Graham Greene, and this, if you will remember, was the period just after the publication of Graham Greene's most noteworthy entertainments. He got me reading these books and, though Greene is often thought of as a pure mystery writer, his tales of suspense and intrigue and crime were the gateway for me to the world of mystery.

"I want to tell you about my friend—about me—and about what we did one summer day back in 1947. . . ."

And then it happened. It happened before Barney's startled eyes.

He had reached over to retrieve the Raven, which he'd set among the other awards not yet claimed. It had occurred to him that the award might be mixed in with the others and somehow escape him. He was clutching it, half-turning back toward Ross Craigthorn, when the road of a gunshot filled the room. He saw the flame leap. He saw it come, it seemed, from the microphone itself, saw it tear into Ross Craigthorn's face and hurl him backward on the raised dais.

Craigthorn staggered, blood already coming from his face and mouth—began to twist, falling against the table. Then he went down, hitting the floor hard. Women were screaming. Men were running toward the platform. The room was in chaos.

Barney Hamet bent over, trying to do something, anything. Betty was at his side, trembling. "Betty, call an ambulance!" he shouted. "Call someone! Quickly!"

"What happened? What happened?"

"Call someone!"

Then he realized that Susan Veldt was also there, pushing through the others, getting to him. "Is he alive?"

For answer, Ross Craigthorn lifted his hand, tried to speak, but only blood came from his mouth where the bullet had entered. His eyes glazed, and in one last desperate lunging effort, he tore at the Raven statuette in Barney Hamet's hand—tore it free and shattered it on the floor of the podium.

Barney tried to speak to him. "Ross! Who did it? What. . . ?"

But there was only more blood, and the life that had remained dribbled fearfully away. The eyes continued to glaze and suddenly were staring at the ceiling. The blood was filling his mouth, running down his cheeks, onto the floor. His body lurched, then was still.

Ross Craigthorn had lived for less than one minute after the bullet tore into his mouth and on to his vital center. Now he was dead.

Somewhere in the room, before three hundred mystery writers and editors, a murderer had struck unseen.

The police came—a brusque detective named George, along with photographers and fingerprint experts and all the others. They came and they examined the body and they listened to the witnesses and they took down names and they photographed angles and they got approximately nowhere.

It was Barney who remembered the microphone and, examining it, noticed that he had seen without noticing earlier—the slim metal tube that was wired to the side of the mike. It was a tube about six inches long, with an empty cartridge inside, and from its back ran two thin copper wires that disappeared into the podium itself. Barney followed the wires down and found a small transistorized unit of some sort inside. He didn't know exactly what it was, but one of the detectives identified it at once.

"Part of one of these two-way citizens' radios. It's a receiving unit actually, set to receive a radio signal."

"A radio signal?" Barney repeated.

By now they were examining the tube and the cartridge. Detective George grunted. "Order the entire thing removed to the back room for further study before being taken to headquarters."

"What do you make of it?" Barney asked.

"Never saw anything like it in my life," the detective told him. He was a big man, with wild hair and a rumpled business suit. He didn't look like a detective, but then he didn't really look like anything else, either.

"This part is just a tube, like they use in zip guns. Basically, the thing is an electrified, radio-controlled zip gun. The cartridge ... I'd guess it to be a thirty-eight—was placed down at the end of this little tube. Some wires were run, and tiny holes drilled right through the cartridge to connect the wires directly with the powder charge. A gap was left between then, enough gap for a spark. When the radio receiving unit was activated, the spark jumped across these terminals, set off the powder charge and propelled the bullet up the tube and out. Very inaccurate, of course. It wouldn't be good at more than five or ten feet, but that's all the distance needed to kill a man here. Naturally he had his face toward the microphone. In this instance he had his mouth right in front of it while he was talking."

"But ... what does it mean? Who set the thing off?" Barney asked.

The detective sighed. "Someone with a unit like this in his possession. It could be hidden in a woman's purse, in a suitcoat pocket, carried almost in the palm of a hand. It would be set to transmit a single signal. When a button was pressed, or a knob turned, it sent its signal and fired the bullet. A very ingenious device, and fairly simple to build."

Barney still could not quite comprehend. "How close would the man have to be to do this?"

"I would guess a few hundred yards. Certainly anyone in

this ballroom could have done it."

"Can you search them?"

But already that seemed hopeless. The guests were scattered. There were some out in the hall, women in the ladies' room, sobbing and hysterical. Several had fainted at the first sight of the blood. Even some men had rushed outside. There was plenty of opportunity for the killer to dispose of his incriminating electronic gear before the police arrived.

"I want the names of everyone here," Detective George said.

"Easy." Barney handed him a list. "There they are. Exactly three hundred and three of them. All you'll need after that are the waiters. I don't know if there was a hotel banquet manager here or not. We had a photographer, too. You'd better get his name."

"Right."

Barney wandered off as if in a daze. Max Winters came running up to him. "This is terrible! Terrible, Barney!"

"You're telling me! I can imagine the headlines tomorrow." He fumbled for a cigarette. "By the way, Max, you would have been the big winner tonight. Congratulations of a sort, I guess."

Max gave a sardonic laugh. "Thanks. I'll pick up my Edgar."

Susan Veldt was there too, and Barney saw rather than comprehended the notebook full of quickly jotted shorthand that she'd been taking down.

Great, he thought. That's all we need right about now.

"Barney . . . what are you going to do?"

"Do they know who did it? Do they know anything at all?"

"They know nothing—except that it was a very cleverly planned crime. A bullet inside a tube, set off by a radio signal from somewhere in this room. All the killer had to do was walk in here this afternoon and tape it to the microphone, and probably nobody noticed him. Or if they did, they didn't pay any attention to him. He just put the receiving unit inside the rostrum, attached the wires, and left. The whole thing would take maybe two minutes at the

56

most—probably less. Sure, wires were visible. The tube was visible. But who was to notice? The only person that would probably have thought it was suspicious would have been an engineer or a loud-speaker expert. Even Craigthorn wouldn't have noticed—they use boom mikes on television. I looked at the thing myself, probably saw it, and never payed any attention to it. You see a couple of extra wires—even a tube attached to the microphone—and you don't think anything of it. Some sort of crazy new electronic gear. What'll they think of next?"

"It's awful, Barney!"

"Murder always is."

"You write about it, but I don't think you ever expected to see it."

"I was a private detective once."

"Did you investigate murders?"

"No. Prosaic things like shoplifting, occasional divorce cases."

"You've had a funny life, Barney."

"Yeah. Ho, ho, A laugh a minute."

"Let's go somewhere for coffee."

"I've got to see the directors. All hell's going to break out around MWA headquarters. Thanks much, but I'll take a raincheck."

"All right," she said.

"I'll call you tomorrow."

He latched onto Max Winters and then hurried on in search of the others. He knew it was going to be a long night. A long night and a long day. "Betty, who else is here among the directors? Bob Fish? Joe Gores? Larry Treat? See who you can round up."

"Right. I'll do the best I can."

Dick McMullen, the agent, came up to him then. "Barney, is there anything I can do?"

"No. Just stand by. That's what I'm telling everybody. Stand by. It's a hell of a night. I've got to get the directors together and decide what we're going to do. It's a hell of a night."

Chapter Eight

SUSAN VELDT

Though the next morning was a Saturday, Susan Veldt was at the offices of *Manhattan* before nine o'clock. She was not surprised to find Arthur Rowe already there, working over proofs for next week's issue. With a weekly magazine that had to make a newsstand appearance every Wednesday and had to reach the printers on Sunday, a great deal of last-minute work was done on Saturday. Susan's own job usually enabled her to do most of the writing earlier in the week. But she knew that Arthur Rowe worked every Saturday, often far into the night, correcting proof, juggling articles to fit, and generally giving each issue the slick appearance that made it all look so easy.

"How are you?" she asked, pausing at the door of his office, tantalizing him because she knew he must be dying to talk to her.

"Sue! My God, Sue! Come in here and tell me all about it! What happened? What happened there? Where were you? How close were you to it? Did you see him get shot? Tell me all about it."

She picked out her favorite chair, a comfortable leather-covered one with brass-studded nails she could run her fingers over. Often the sessions in Arthur Rowe's office lasted for hours, and it gave her something to do. This morning, though, she was eager to talk. The night before had been an experience, not just because it was the first time she'd ever seen anyone murdered, but because, happening where it did in the midst of all those celebrities, it had taken on the aspects of a thunderbolt. It was as if she had seen an act of God. There'd been a bullet fired without any hand on a trigger.

She ran quickly over the night's events, recounting them in detail, as Rowe made occasional notes on his ubiquitous pad. He chomped so tightly on the pipe that she thought he might bit it through. Finally he took it from his mouth and placed it in the overflowing ashtray.

"Sue, we've got something here! We've got something damn big! And I'm not going to let it get away from us. There are murders every day in Manhattan, but this murder is going to make our magazine."

"What do you mean, Chief?" As well as "Boss," she called him "Chief" sometimes, and he never seemed to mind. Maybe it made him feel like an Indian. Today he didn't even notice—nor did he notice her nyloned legs where the skirt rested four inches above her crossed knees. He really was fired up today. Not even time for her legs.

"This is what I mean, Sue. We have Ross Craigthorn, one of the most popular, best-known television personalities in the country, an ace newsman, murdered. Murdered in the sight of three hundred people. And this is the topper: those people were not just anybody. Those people were mystery writers, mystery editors, agents. It's their job to try and tantalize the public with the solving of crimes—their job to create detectives, and murderers, and all the rest of the hokum. Don't you see? What will happen now? Will the Mystery Writers of America band together to solve this murder in their midst? And if they do, or if they don't, we've got a story either way. Just think of it . . . *MWA helpless before murder at Awards Dinner*. Or, *MWA sets out to capture killer on its own*. And if they do set out, Sue, what happens? Either they find him, or they don't. And either way, we've got the story of the year! You can write it as satire, or black comedy, or any way you want—but we've got a great story! *Mystery writers fail to catch mur-*

derer. Or maybe, *Mystery writers track down murderer when police fail*. Either way, it sells copies."

Susan Veldt looked dubious. "Are you turning *Manhattan* into a true-crime magazine, Chief?"

"I'm turning it into whatever this damn town of ours is, Sue. Some weeks it's tragedy—other weeks it's humor. Some weeks, like last year, we devoted the entire issue to the funeral of Robert Kennedy. Another week, like this spring, we have a strike. Every day is different here. Snowstorms and plane crashes and who knows what. This week we've got a murder, and I think it's going to last us for a good many weeks. From what you've told me about this deadly little device, our killer was no amateur. In fact, he sounds like a mystery writer himself, to dream up an infernal machine like that."

"All right," she said. "I'm convinced. What do you want me to do?" If she wasn't entirely convinced, she knew that he was, and after all, he was the boss and she was the employee, and it was a job—a job she liked.

"Here's what I want you to do. What's that guy's name? The guy you were with last night?"

"Barney Hamet."

"Tell me something about him."

"It's in my first article, resting in your *In* box, if you ever get around to looking at your *In* box."

He shuffled through some papers until he found it. "It's too long to read now. Tell me about it anyway."

"He's a sometime writer. For a while he was a private detective. Now he's executive vice president of MWA."

"What about his personal life? Married?"

"Single now. I think he was divorced or something."

"Good looking guy? Go for a girl like you?"

She ran a casual hand over her nylons. "I guess."

"Fine. Stick to him. Do whatever you have to, Sue girl. But stick to him. He's going to be your meal ticket. I want to know everything that MWA does on this case. I want to know if they're going to leave it in the police hands, if they're going to try and find the killer themselves, if they're going to just try and shovel it under the rug. Whatever they do, you go with them and find out, and keep that typewriter hot. We're going to have the story of the year! This is the kind of thing *Manhattan* was made for!"

"Do you really think it's fair to be satirical about a man's murder? Don't you think the public might object to us making fun of one more bit of violence?"

"We're not making fun of the violence. We're not making fun of Ross Craigthorn. We only might—just might—have a little fun at the expense of MWA. That is, if they decide to play detective and make a botch of it."

"All right," she sighed. "I guess you know best."

"That's why I'm the editor."

She left him and went back to her typewriter and stared at it for a long time. Finally she put a sheet of paper in and started typing up last night's events, running over much of the same material that she had already told Rowe, but clarifying things in her own mind. At one point she had a thought, and flipped on the intercom.

"Mr. Rowe, this is Sue. What about the rest of the series? We've got the Pulitzer awards coming up the first week in May."

He thought for a moment, then snapped back, "Put someone else on it! You stay on this mystery writers' thing!"

"Right, Chief."

She went back to her typewriter, thinking a little about Barney Hamet and how she would approach him.

Chapter Nine

BARNEY HAMET

MWA headquarters, above the restaurant off Times Square, was a scene of saddened energy at three o'clock Saturday afternoon. It was the hour for the regular director's meeting, and though there had been some talk of canceling or postponing it, Barney had finally decided that it must be held. There were just so many things to be gone over—statements to the press, letters to members, an article to be written for next month's *Third Degree*, the MWA house organ.

Barney stood at the head of the directors' table and looked down at the score of assembled members. They always had a better crowd after the annual dinner, if only because so many of the directors were from out of town, like Max Winters. He had to travel all the way from California, something he could hardly do for every monthly meeting. But now they were here, and it was a good time to air old problems and list new ones.

"All right," Barney said. "So we've got ourselves a murder. A front-page murder at that. You people have seen the *Times* and the *News*. The *Post* this afternoon plays it up big too. We're on the spot in one hell of a way. A famous person has been killed at our Awards Dinner and you know where that leaves us? Right behind the eight ball! We're damned if we do, and damned if we don't!"

"Do or don't what?" Max Winters asked from down the table, next to Clayton Rawson. "Why do we have to do anything?"

"Well, we don't really. But I know some of those fancy writers will be on us. The whole thing just makes us look foolish. It wasn't as if he had just been shot or stabbed. He had to be killed with some crazy device that looks like it was dreamed up by a mystery writer some night after a few gin-and-tonics." He looked down the table to where Betty Rafferty sat making quick shorthand notes. "Betty, you were as close to him as I was. Did you see anything?"

"Not a thing, Barney . . . except how he took that Raven out of your hand and smashed it. We'll have to get you a new one."

"I'm not worried about that right now. I'm mainly worried about why he did it."

"A dying message . . ." Max Winters said, giving words to the obvious.

"Sure. A dying message." Barney sighed and looked down, scratching his head. "Don't think I haven't given it a lot of concentration. I even called Fred Dannay up in Larchmont this morning." Dannay was one half of the Ellery Queen writing combination, and a number of his plots, especially in the short-short length, had concerned dying messages.

"I called Fred and talked to him for half an hour. We discussed the thing up and down and inside out. He agrees it was a dying message of some sort, but he's as puzzled by it as the rest of us. Raven—bird—maybe some other bird. Maybe the killer's name has a bird in it. There was no other bird around except for the Raven's statue, so he grabbed for the closest thing handy. There are a dozen explanations and we've got nothing to go on."

Betty Rafferty spoke up from the end of the table. "I've gone through the entire guest list. There's not a bird among them."

Harry Fox, being only an associate member, was not formally part of the board of directors, but he often dropped in on meetings, and he sat over near the makeshift bar now, voicing occasional comments. "I'm a Fox. That's an animal. Does that help any?"

"Afraid not," Barney said.

"Well," Max spoke up. "At least we know one thing. The Raven wasn't filled with jewels and gold like Sam Spade's falcon."

"Now, Max," Barney reminded him. "That falcon was fake, made out of lead, if I remember right."

"What do we do?" someone else asked. "Let's cut the chatter and get down to business."

What they did for the next half hour was listen to opinions—from Jim Reach and Chris Steinbrunner, Gloria Armoury and Aaron Marc Stein. The opinions brought up various points, and took off in various directions, but the sum of it was that nobody knew exactly what to do. They all agreed that MWA had to come out of it looking good. There was too much at stake in the organization's prestige.

"It's like that time a few years ago," Max Winters said, reminding them all of another turbulent dispute when a convicted murderer had written a mystery novel, then applied for membership in MWA while he awaited execution. "Remember the fight we had that time? Finally we decided we just couldn't let him in."

"It's not like that at all," Barney said. "This thing is different. I don't think it was even an MWA member who killed him. The place was full of editors, agents, any number of people. There were even some radio and TV people there. Maybe they had a reason to do away with him."

"The thing to do is check all the names on that seating list," Harry Fox said. "Every one of them. Find out how much they knew about Craigthorn. Maybe we'll turn up a bitter enemy first time out."

Barney nodded in agreement. "I'm going to ask you all to work on this with me. I'm going to give you a few names each and start you digging."

"One thing," Max said. "Barney, you're a detective. You were a licensed private eye for a good many years, and you're known as such. You're our executive vice president, besides. Barney, I think MWA should hire you formally, or informally, to investigate Craigthorn's murder."

"I haven't been a detective for years, Max. You know that."

"But you can get back into the swing of things. Look, Barney, you're the logical one. A lot of mystery writers running off half-cocked aren't going to get anywhere. At least you've had investigative experience. You know the sort of things that we need to find. If you don't find them, okay, but nobody can criticize us if we have you looking for them. Do you still have a license in New York State?"

"No," Barney said. "I let it lapse years ago."

"It doesn't matter. You're the one for it, Barney."

"What about that girl?" Betty Rafferty asked. "Is she going to make trouble? The writer from *Manhattan* magazine?"

Barney had forgotten Susan Veldt for the moment, although he knew he shouldn't have. "I don't know. What do you want me to do with her? Take her to bed with me?"

Max Winters chuckled. "It wouldn't be a bad idea. For the good of the organization, and all that stuff. You might even enjoy yourself."

"I don't know." Barney thought about it—about Susan Veldt a little, but mostly about what the directors were asking him to do. "There's not a clue in it anywhere. We've got more than three hundred suspects—anyone in that room. We've got even maybe twenty or so waiters. Besides which, just about anybody in the city could have walked in there without being noticed, the way people were shuffling around."

"But we have a list of the prime suspects," Max reminded him. "This guest list right here. With the seating arrangements and all. Maybe the police will be able to pin down that radio gadget a little better. Maybe they'll say the killer had to be within twenty feet—or ten feet. If so, that would narrow down the suspects right away."

Barney shook his head. "They're not going to say that. If they were going to say anything along those lines, they'd have said it already. No—we're stuck with a murder that could have been committed by anybody in that room. Damned ingenious device, too. I wish I'd have used it in one of my books."

"You'll work on the case?" Harry Fox asked.

"I'll look around for a day or two," Barney agreed. "And I'll try and get this gal off our necks. I'm not pretending to be any sort of detective, though. It's for the police to find out who killed him. We can help a bit, that's all."

Harry had another idea. "How about this all-night radio show tomorrow? Are we going on with it as planned?"

Barney had completely forgotten Skinny Simon's proposal in the rush of events. "What do you think?"

"I think we should do it," Harry said. "It's important to us now. We can get our message across to the people, maybe even appeal for some sort of help. But I think you should be on the show with the rest of us, Barney—especially if you're undertaking the investigation. It would give us a peg for the whole discussion."

Max Winters was far from certain, though. "What if Skinny Simon says something about violence being encouraged by mysteries? About all the violence on television and movies, and all the murders in our books?"

"Well, hell, Max! Someone will say that anyway, and we might as well be there to defend ourselves. Right?" This came from Harry Fox.

Barney interrupted before things got too heated. "Okay. I'll do it. You two guys are going on the show?"

"Right."

"We still need two others."

Max spoke up. "We've got two others. Dick McMullen will do it. I think he's anxious to stay on my good side and get back to being my agent. Then I've got another one lined up too. I haven't been sleeping all morning, you know. Frank Jesset—the confession magazine editor. That friend of Ross Craigthorn's."

"Friend?" Betty asked. "They weren't looking too friendly when I saw them last night."

"Okay," Max said. "So maybe we'll have the murderer right there with us. Craigthorn brought two people with him—his secretary, Miss Sweeney, and Frank Jesset. Maybe he's been shacking up with Miss Sweeney all these years and Jesset wanted a piece of the action. Maybe Jesset rigged that thing up to kill him. Who knows? Barney—I'll bet if you play your cards right you can get a confession out of him right on Skinny Simon's show."

"Sure, sure," Barney said.

They ran through some routine business and then adjourned to the makeshift bar.

The Awards Dinner was traditionally followed by a cocktail party, and although they played it down after the previous night's events, they hadn't entirely canceled it. A few members drifted in—not so much to drink as to commiserate with the others. It was a great night for commiserating.

Barney was standing by the front window around seven o'clock looking out at the busy evening street when he saw Susan Veldt crossing over and coming in the downstairs door.

All right, he decided. This is where it starts. Whatever I'm going to do to the girl—sock her or seduce her—will start tonight.

He turned and put on his brightest smile as he walked to the door to greet her.

Chapter Ten

SUSAN VELDT

She had never seen such a place—smoky and crowded and gloomily detached. It seemed entirely different from the small, somewhat cheerless library she'd visited earlier in the week. The people made the difference, she decided, but she could not determine whether it was a difference for the better or worse. All she knew was that it was crowded and smoky—and Barney Hamet was already pressing a cold drink into her hand.

"Scotch and water. I hope it's your brand," he said.

She wondered what he was up to. "Thanks. I thought you might cancel the cocktails in view of last night's events."

"This is basically a pretty private affair and we're just talking things over. We didn't encourage any outsiders to come in. Actually it's just about over. Could I interest you in dinner afterwards?"

She glanced at her watch. "Well, I was planning to wash my hair and write a few letters."

"Hair-washing and letter-writing are for nights when there's nothing else swinging. You want to stay a bachelor gal for the rest of your life?"

She laughed a bit and gave in easily. "All right, dinner it is. But didn't you promise to phone me today?"

"I was busy every minute. I'll tell you about it."

They didn't stay too much longer, only time enough for her to get a general impression of the people—somber, worried, talking, of course, about the previous night's events. Several of them had late editions of the afternoon paper, and they were browsing through the columns of the *Post* to see what had been said about the MWA murder case. Happily, the reporting was straight and factual. No one had taken any digs at the obvious object of satire. People were, perhaps, still too dulled and sickened by the violence which had claimed a man as famous and popular as Ross Craigthorn. It would be another week or ten days before the humorous aspects, if that was the word for them, began to bob above the surface of people's minds. Another ten days—just about the time that *Manhattan* hit the stands.

She wondered if Arthur Rowe would try to get something in this week's issue, and decided he would not. It would have meant editing her copy almost on the spot, for his printers' deadline. He'd be more likely to watch her stuff as it came in every day and weave a good article out of it for the following week's issue. By that time, too, the horror of Craigthorn's killing would have subsided into the background and the whole thing would be ripe for a razor-sharp satirical slant.

They left MWA headquarters around eight o'clock and decided to eat nearby. They crossed the street to the Absinthe House and ordered something there. The food was good and the atmosphere pleasant, and she found herself relaxing and actually enjoying it, even though she couldn't quite figure what Barney Hamet had in mind.

"Tell me about yourself," he said. "You know—the real you."

"The real me! There is no real me. What do you want me to tell you? About all my old boyfriends? About how I'm a career girl? That sort of thing?"

"I suppose. Where do you live, for instance?"

"Opposite Central Park—above the zoo. I can hear the lions every night."

"And the wolves?" he asked with a chuckle.

"Those too. Sometimes I hear ambulances—and I always hear parades. It's that sort of an apartment."

"It's that sort of a city," he said.

"And what about you, the famous Barney Hamet? I must admit I read one of your books the other day. It was called *A Place to Die*. I have another one, *The Shadow Woman*, but I haven't had a chance to read it yet."

"I don't write much anymore. Those are the only two novels I ever did. I write a few short stories when I have a chance. Had one in *Ellery Queen's Mystery Magazine* last month, but it was one he bought a year ago."

"Tell me about this murder," she asked finally, over dessert.

"What's there to tell? The man is dead and I suppose somebody there killed him. I sure don't know who, though."

"No ideas?"

"No ideas."

"It would be sort of funny if it was one of you mystery writers."

"It wasn't one of us mystery writers. I don't think there was an MWA member in that room who would have committed a crime under those circumstances. I'd be willing to bet on it. I'll lay you twelve to one . . ."

"Twelve to one? Good! That's my lunch hour," she said. It was a line she'd heard from a girl once. She'd been saving it all these years for just the right spot.

He eyed her a bit uncertainly, chuckled, then lit a cigarette. "Wise gal, aren't you? Career gal. New York gal."

"Aren't we all?"

"Huh! How's your dessert?"

She stirred the melting ice cream in her dish. "Okay."

"Want an after-dinner drink?"

"I could use one, I guess. A grasshopper, please."

He ordered two grasshoppers, and when they came he seemed to relax a bit. He was eyeing her over the green drink, perhaps trying to figure her out.

She decided she could almost read his mind. It wasn't difficult at all. Maybe she could have a little fun with him. She hadn't had any real fun with a man in quite a while.

"Where to now?" he asked. "I know a nice place in the Village."

"I know a nice place opposite the park," she countered.

"That would be up around where you live, wouldn't it?"

"Around there."

"Okay. Let's grab a cab. What floor are you on?"

"High. Up high. The tenth floor."

"Good. I always wanted to see the Central Park Zoo from ten floors up."

They took a cab uptown and she was surprised to find that it was already ten-thirty when they reached her apartment.

"Come on up," she said, casually, as if that had not been both their intentions.

They rode the elevator in silence, and she wondered what he was thinking; she wondered, and of course, knew. He wasn't the first one who'd accompanied her up there like this, but she hoped somehow this would be better than it was with the silk-shirted ad man who didn't even remember her name.

"An after-after-dinner drink," she said. "Just what we both need."

He glanced around the apartment, taking in the modern art reproductions and a few originals. "Who painted this one?" he asked, studying an impressionistic Manhattan skyline.

"A fellow I know who's an art director at Walter Thompson. He's good, don't you think?"

"Good, yes. I don't know if I approve his choice of colors, though."

"Let me slip into something comfortable," she said. "Then I'll make us the drinks."

"I've heard that line before."

She came out wearing a Chinese hostess gown she'd received as a gift the Christmas before last. She remembered the day she'd opened the box and seen it, a gift from her sister in Chicago, and wondered what in hell she'd ever do with it. Tonight it seemed just right. It was loose, flowing, and covered with squirming yellow dragons.

"Any choice? Scotch all right?"

"Scotch would be perfect," Barney said.

"So I told you about myself. Now it's your turn."

71

"When did you tell me about yourself? You didn't tell me a thing about yourself, except that you work for that foolish magazine."

"And all I know about you is that you're a private detective."

"*Was* a private detective."

"And you're going to solve Ross Craigthorn's murder."

"Sure. Sure I am." He came over to where she was mixing the drinks, and kissed her lightly on the neck.

"That tickled," she said softly.

"It was supposed to."

She stirred the drinks a little more vigorously than necessary and handed his to him. She'd laced it well with a double shot of Scotch and very little water.

"You make a good drink."

"Thank you, sir."

"This is a nice place. How many rooms?"

"This one. The bedroom. The bath. That's all. It goes for a fancy figure, but I think it's worth it for entertaining. A nice neighborhood. Right in the next block is one of the most expensive co-op apartments in New York City."

He grunted and downed his Scotch. "Come sit by me," he suggested, and she took him up on the offer. "I haven't necked with a girl since high school."

"That's hard to believe."

"Well, I won't say I haven't done anything else with them, but I haven't necked with them." He kissed her lightly and ran his hand over her breast. She responded immediately, pausing only to turn out the nearest light so that the whole of the room was bathed in a soft, subdued glow.

"Let me fix you another drink first," she said.

"All right, I'll take you up on that."

She came back in a moment with the drink and then let her hand drop casually in his lap and ran it up the inside of his thigh.

"You're a fast worker," he said.

"No time like the present."

After five minutes of further fumbling on the sofa, he suggested they go to bed.

72

"Let me slip out of this thing," she told him. "It's a present from my sister in Chicago, and I don't want to rip the dragons."

"Fair enough." He followed her into the darkened bedroom. "What kind of an article are you going to write for that magazine of yours?"

She half turned toward him. "Oh, something about what a great lover Barney Hamet is, I suppose. How would that be? Build up your ego?"

"Stop kidding. You're the damndest kidder I ever saw."

"Well, take off your clothes for God's sake! You're not going to get into my bed with all those clothes on."

"Where? Here?"

"In the bathroom."

"All right."

She tossed the hostess gown aside, draping it over a chair, and slid under the covers. Although it was April, she pulled the quilt up to her shoulders and waited for him.

He came out finally, naked except for a pair of white jockey shorts that clung to his middle. He had a nice build, and she admired that in a man. His legs were long and firm and just a little bit hairy. In the dim light from the living room, he reminded her of the first one—the college boy at the fraternity party.

That was when she started to freeze up.

"What's wrong?" he asked, starting toward the bed.

"I . . . nothing."

He pulled the shorts down around his ankles and stepped out of them. "Don't worry. I'm gentle."

"Close the door. There's so much light."

He did as she requested, and then came back, lifting the quilt to slip beneath it. "You're shivering."

"Yes."

"Why?"

"I don't know. I guess I don't do this every day." Then, "You want me to write a nice article about you, don't you?"

"That has nothing to do with this."

She turned away from him in the bed. "I . . ."

"What in hell's the matter with you, anyway?"

"I'm sorry, Barney. I can't."

73

"Look, this has nothing to do with any article! This is just between you and me."

"I'm sorry, Barney," she said, getting out of bed. "You'll have to leave."

"Are you human or what?"

She picked up the dragon-covered robe and slipped into it. "I'm human, Barney. Too human, I guess. I keep thinking of that damned article and I freeze up. I don't want you like this, as part of a deal of some sort. Maybe later, when this is all over."

"There won't be any later," he growled.

"Could I get you another drink?"

"I don't want anything from you," he said. He picked up his shorts and slipped into them and retrieved the rest of his clothes from the bathroom. "I don't want a thing from you."

He finished knotting his tie in a crude bulge and slipped on his suit coat. "Boy . . . the girls you meet in this world!"

"Barney—maybe it'll be better the next time."

"I won't count on it."

She watched him cross the living room and slam the door and then she poured herself a stiff shot of Scotch. She went to the window and looked down at animals in the park, and had some more Scotch, and then cried a little, and went to bed.

Chapter Eleven

BARNEY HAMET

He took a taxi back to his apartment, full of a fury he'd never known could grip him, thinking of all the things he should have done, the things he should have said.

"This is your place, mister," the taxi driver said.

"Yeah." Barney gave him a big tip and went up. Saturday night in New York.

He switched on the one o'clock news, but there was nothing new on Ross Craigthorn, just the fact that funeral services would be held Monday. Monday seemed a long way off. Then he remembered the radio show the following night. He should sleep late in the morning—have at least a few of his wits about him for the thing.

Occasionally, back in the old days, he'd have gone to church on a Sunday morning, but now that was a rarity, like a lot of other things in his past. He started to set the alarm for nine o'clock, then decided to just sleep as long as he could. Sunday night was going to be a long one.

He didn't remember dreaming, although at one point in the night it seemed that Susan Veldt might have come to him. But that was probably a nightmare.

He woke, rolled over and looked at the clock and saw that it was ten minutes to ten. Well, almost eight hours.

He couldn't expect any more than that, not with losing an hour to the start of Daylight Savings Time.

He remembered her again, as he poured some orange juice. He remembered what had happened the night before. He thought about calling her, decided against it, but then did it anyway after breakfast.

"Hello," she said, all sweetness. Maybe she was expecting her boss, or her lover, or her mother, or her sister in Chicago.

"Hello."

"Who is this?"

"A fellow named Barney Hamet. Spent a little time with you last night."

"Oh, Barney! I really didn't expect to hear from you—not this soon at least. You're calling to tell me you've cracked the Craigthorn murder case!"

"No." He had a sudden impulse. "I want you to spend tonight with me."

"Tonight?" she asked a little uncertainly, not understanding what he meant.

"Yeah, tonight. I'm going to be on an all-night radio show, Skinny Simon's show, with some of the other writers. Great chance for you to stay up late. Get rid of all your frustrations. Drink black coffee and listen to all us mystery writers kick around the Craigthorn murder case. How about it?"

"Well . . . would I be on the show?"

"I'll get you a set in the control booth. Nice padded chair next to the engineer. You can feel him up if things get dull."

"You're a bastard, Barney!"

"Sorry. I didn't mean that."

She was silent a moment. Then, "All right, I'll come. What time?"

"I'm not going to offer to pick you up at your apartment. You know where Skinny's station is?"

"I'll find it."

"Okay. Meet me there at eleven-thirty. I've got to round up some other people and make sure they show. These days I don't trust anybody. Max Winters is probably off on a ben-

76

der and heaven knows where the rest are. One of them is a friend of Craigthorn's, and I haven't even talked to him about it yet."

"All right." She hesitated and then added, "I'm sorry about last night, Barney . . . sorry it worked out that way, anyhow."

"Sure. See you tonight."

He hung up and stared at the phone for a minute. He wasn't about to be seduced or induced or reduced by this girl again. It was all business from here on in.

He called the MWA number, but of course Betty wasn't there on a Sunday. He finally reached her at her apartment and suggested she come to the studio that night for a while. "You can serve coffee and make notes and things, Betty, and if somebody doesn't show up, maybe you can fill in."

She was a bit hesitant at this. "I'm no good on the radio—not with my voice. And I'm sure not going to stay up all night listening to you guys talk."

"Any idea where Max Winters is?"

"Probably at his hotel. Have you tried there?"

"Not yet. Look—how about these other people that are supposed to be on the show? Frank Jesset? Do you know how to reach him? And Dick McMullen?"

"Jesset?"

"You know—that friend of Craigthorn's. Max seemed to think he was going to be on."

"All right, I'll try to reach him," she said. "I gather Harry is all set. He seemed to know the details."

He hung up and headed for Max's hotel. He was in his room, all right, but he wasn't alone. Detective George, the big man in the rumpled suit from Friday night, was there with him.

"Well, well," George said, getting to his feet. "It's Mr. Hamet again. Nice to see you. Mr. Winters here was just telling me you're going to be doing some investigating on the case."

"Strictly off the record," Barney hastened to inform him. "I used to be a private detective. They think I might be useful, more as a public relations expert than as a sleuth,

77

though."

George nodded. "I've been talking to Mr. Winters about his recollection of what happened."

Max sat in his chair, smoking a cigarette and looking just a bit bored. "What's there to say? I've gone over the story five times already. I didn't know Craigthorn. I never even watched his television show. He was there and he got shot and now he's dead, but my plane leaves for California tomorrow and this is a whole other world for me, this New York."

George frowned at him. "They don't have murders in California, Mr. Winters? I seem to remember Senator Kennedy getting killed out in Los Angeles just last year."

"Sure, they have murders. And they have cops, too. I write about them all the time. But New York is still a different thing. You're all in a hurry here. I think you're all in a hurry to die."

"Not on the freeways, at least," the detective said. "I think I'm about finished with you though. Uh . . . do you have a few moments, Mr. Hamet? I wonder if I could take you downstairs and buy you a cup of coffee in the lobby."

Barney saw no way out of it. "Max, you're all set for the radio show tonight?"

"Sure am."

"Right. We're supposed to be at the studio around eleven-thirty. I'll see you there."

He rode down on the elevator with Detective George, exchanging casual pleasantries about the weather, which was warm but clouding over.

"Last Sunday in April. I always hope for good weather this time of the year," George said. "The picnics up in Central Park . . ."

"You live in the city?"

"Yeah. Got a wife and family. I hated to get up this morning, what with losing an hour. I generally have Sundays off, except when there's a case like this. With Craigthorn getting killed, we've got ten extra men working on the thing."

Barney nodded sympathetically because there was nothing to say.

In the coffee shop, he stirred some sugar into his coffee and waited for the detective's questions.

"So you were a private eye, huh? I don't think that I ever really met one. It's a heck of an admission for a detective to make. You know, we travel pretty much in different circles. I've usually been assigned to midtown here. Never really got to know any of you fellas."

"I like to think of myself as a writer now," Barney said.

"Yeah. I read your last book. That was a pretty sexy cover they had on it."

"I don't do the cover art."

"No, of course not. I didn't mean to offend you." He sipped his coffee. "What do you think about this thing? Who do you think killed Craigthorn?"

"I'm pretty sure it was not a member of MWA. This gimmick with the bullet being fired electrically from a pipe taped to a microphone—it's too much like the sort of thing some clever murderer would imagine some equally clever author dreaming up. I think the whole gimmick was just a plot to kill Craigthorn and put the blame on our organization."

"You think anyone would really want to do that? Why, Mr. Hamet?"

"Not mainly to discredit the organization—but just to throw attention away from the real killer. There were a lot of non-writers at the dinner Friday night. Even some friends of Craigthorn's."

"Yeah. You probably mean the secretary, Miss . . . ah . . ." He flipped through his notebook, then came up with the name. "Yeah, Miss Sweeney. She's sort of a looker. You think he was sleeping with her?"

"I'm sure I've told you I didn't know the man."

"Somebody at MWA must have known him to choose him for the award. This Reader of the Year thing."

"I guess so," Barney admitted. "Harry Fox, one of our associate members, gets around town, sees a lot of people. He probably suggested it to the board of directors. Craigthorn was well known for his television show."

"What about this friend that came with him—Frank Jesset? He's some sort of an editor, isn't he?"

"True confessions magazine, from what I understand," Barney said. "A few of our people write for them—not too many. They pay a little, but since the stories are supposed to be true they're never signed. There's something about anonymity that doesn't appeal to most authors. It wouldn't appeal to me anyway."

George grunted and tried to smooth down his wild hair. "So you've got no ideas about the thing? You were pretty sharp finding that electrical device in the podium."

"I was standing right next to him when he was shot. It wasn't too difficult to see where the bullet came from."

"What about this statuette he pulled out of your hand? This Raven thing?"

"Well, it's an award, a non-writing award given by MWA. You saw it. You saw what it looked like."

"Why did he pull it out of your hand?"

"He was obviously trying to tell me something—perhaps to name his murderer. I don't know."

"There was no *Raven* at the dinner. There was no bird of any sort. There wasn't even anybody named *Eagle* or *Hawk* or *Crow* or *Robin*. We checked the girls; *Robin,* you know, is sort of a nickname, but there weren't any, Mr. Hamet."

"Have you dug into his past? Something on his news show, perhaps? Something in politics? A political assassination?" They were pretty farfetched suggestions, but at this point Barney was throwing out anything that came to mind.

"No. It seems to be a more personal type of slaying. A political assassin usually walks up to the victim and pulls a gun and shoots him, or else maybe uses a high-powered rifle. They don't go for all this jazz with radio signals firing bullets. That's a little more personal."

Barney lit a cigarette. "Have you considered the possibility that Craigthorn was not the intended victim? That this device misfired at the wrong moment?"

"Well, who was the intended victim then?" the detective wanted to know. "The awards were kept fairly confidential, as I understand it, all except the one to Craigthorn. I doubt if any outsider would even have known that Harry Fox was going to give his little talk. They certainly wouldn't have known that people like Max Winters were going to win. You were the only one definitely scheduled to speak, outside of Craigthorn. Are you telling us the bullet was meant for you?"

Barney could not in all honesty tell him that. "I don't know who it was meant for. I suppose it was meant for Craigthorn. A killer as clever as this one wouldn't have fired the thing at the wrong moment."

"I hear you're having a little all-night radio session tonight."

Barney nodded. "Skinny Simon's show. Listen in."

"I can't stay up all night listening to the radio. The wife would think I was some sort of a nut. You tell me if anything exciting happens."

Barney nodded. "I'll do that."

"And if you get any tips on the case, pass them along to me. We're always happy to have some extra help."

"Right."

Barney left him in the coffee shop and headed back to his own apartment. Maybe he could catch a few hours' sleep before the appearance on Skinny's show. At least he could try.

The studios of WJON were in a building just south of Times Square, one of those nondescript office buildings that was not tall enough or new enough or modern enough to attract more than a passing glance. Tourists sometimes mistook it for part of the garment district, though that was several blocks further to the south. This building held the usual assortment of offices—a bank on the ground floor, a few lawyers, an insurance agency, a theatrical booking agent and, as one neared the top, three floors given over to the studios of WJON radio.

In a city with as many radio stations as New York, it was theoretically possible for someone to spend most of his existence without ever happening upon Simon's all-night talk show, but for those who did, the experience was not to be quickly forgotten. Skinny Simon's voice, for one thing, came through on the radio in a deep, demanding tone, completely unlike his physical body, which lacked its authority. It was possible that Skinny was made for radio. He certainly was not made for television, where one look at his sagging frame and drooping eyelids gave many Friday-night viewers the shudders. Though he was not as thin as he had been when he acquired his nickname back in college, he gave the impression of being always in motion, like a runner or a high-jumper, with arms sometimes actually waving as he talked.

During the MWA dinner he had been fairly well in control of himself, but now in his own bailiwick Barney saw him in full flight.

"Barney! Barney! Glad you could make it! What time is it?"

"Almost eleven-thirty."

"Where the hell are the rest of those guys?"

"Who's here so far?"

"Just Harry Fox. *God*—I thought you were going to have five people here for me."

"They'll be here—don't worry. You've got a half-hour till show time," Barney reassured him, following along into a large, drag studio with a control booth at one end.

The engineer was there, but neither Susan Veldt nor Betty had made an appearance as yet.

"Some detective was here questioning me a while ago," Skinny said.

"A fellow named George?"

"Yeah. I guess that was the name. What are they doing—going down the whole guest list?"

"I suppose so," Barney said. "Did you know Craigthorn?"

"I never laid eyes on him, except at a few cocktail parties. You know—broadcasting affairs—things like that. I maybe said two words to him in `my life—hello and goodbye. He wasn't the friendly sort."

Barney remembered Skinny's attempt to speak with Ross at the dinner, but he decided not to press the point.

Skinny Simon's white leather swivel chair was on one side of an oval table. The other five chairs were arranged facing him, each with its own microphone. Barney couldn't help glancing down the line of mikes for any extraneous wires or tubes, but there were none.

"Well, we go on the air in twenty-five minutes. I hope those guys show." He went back out to the hall, and Barney walked into the control room, looking for Harry Fox.

He finally found him bent over a drinking fountain, taking a pill of some sort—perhaps to quiet his nerves, or to keep him awake.

"How are you Harry? How's our expert tonight?"

"Not feeling very expert, Barney. Heartburn. I should be home in bed. If I hadn't promised to do this thing, I probably would be."

"Did you get a visit from a detective today?"

Harry shook his head. "No, not yet. Why? Are they checking everybody out?"

"Sounds like it."

Harry dropped the little vial of pills into his pocket. "Well, here comes Max and his would-be agent. Let's go meet them."

Dick McMullen had his arm around Max's shoulder, probably telling him about all the thousands of dollars he was going to make in the coming year. Maybe a big movie sale just around the corner, or a television series that might pan out for the season after the season after next. That was the way agents like McMullen worked. But Barney had to admit he wasn't really a bad guy.

Then he saw Susan Veldt getting off the elevator and coming toward the station reception desk. He walked over to meet her. "Good evening. I didn't know if you'd make it."

"I made it," she said. "How are you, Barney?"

"I had a good night's sleep. Feel a lot better today."

"Glad to hear it."

They walked back to the studio, and Barney got her seated in the control room in a worn chair with the stuffing sticking out of its arms and back.

"There, you can get a view of the whole thing, and make all the notes you want for your magazine."

"Thanks," she said.

"Fifteen minutes to air time!" Skinny said. "Who are we missing? Jesset? Jesset, is it? Is that the guy's name? Who is he? Who is he?"

"A confession editor, friend of Craigthorn's. I guess

somebody thought you might want to talk about the murder."

"Yeah. Yeah. I want to talk about the murder," Skinny said. "Just wish he'd show up."

Betty Rafferty came in then, bearing coffee for all assembled. She was efficient, even at midnight on a Sunday.

A few minutes later Frank Jesset arrived. Miss Sweeney, Craigthorn's secretary, was with him. Someone dragged another chair out of an office so all three of the ladies could sit in the control room. But it was obvious that Skinny did not care for this much of an audience.

"What have you got? The whole cheering section out there, Barney?"

"You know how it is, Skinny. Our love life. I doubt if any of them will stay past the first hour. They all look pretty sleepy now."

"Yeah." Skinny ran through a few preliminary instructions, telling them not to touch the microphone during the show, not to speak too closely into it, to be natural, to watch profanity, to watch for his hand signals. "It's a long night till five in the morning, but we'll take a break about three-thirty—get some food for you folks," he said. "Okay?"

They nodded.

Jesset was looking progressively more disturbed as each minute passed. He was probably wishing he was home in bed, with Miss Sweeney.

The engineer cued Skinny, and at the stroke of twelve he started his pitch. "The Skinny Simon Show! Brought to you, each and every night at this time through the facilities of W-J-O-N in New—York—City!"

Barney listened to the rest of the spiel, familiar with it, because he had heard it maybe once a week for the last several years. Skinny was an institution. The show was on each night of the week, although only five nights of it were live. The other two were usually taped repeats of some previous shows.

Skinny shifted into high gear. "*Five* outstanding mystery writers, editors, agents, experts in all things mysterious! And we're going to talk about a number of subjects tonight—not the least of which will be the tragic death of television news commentator Ross Craigthorn just two nights ago at the annual dinner of Mystery Writers of America.

"Now, introducing our guests, we have Barney Hamet, executive vice president of MWA; Max Winters, mystery novelist, and winner of this year's Edgar Award for the best novel of the year, *The Fox Hunt*; Harry Fox, who is not the fox being hunted, but is rather an expert on all things mysterious, including the early history of the whodunit; Dick McMullen, an author's agent, one of the most successful in the business; and Frank Jesset, magazine editor, and close personal friend of Ross Craigthorn.

"Well, fellows, we're here for the night and I suppose we might as well get right down to cases. Before we get into a lengthy discussion of MWA and its goals and achievements over these past twenty-odd years, I know our listeners would want to know if there has been any progress in the hunt for Ross Craigthorn's slayer. Barney—speaking as executive vice president, do you have anything to offer on that subject?"

Barney cleared his throat a little too loudly, knowing that it must have boomed out the microphone. He shoved back in his chair a few inches and said, "Nothing really new. We're working on it. The police are working on it. We're doing a little personal investigative work and any results that we find will immediately be turned over to the police. I know that every one of us is shocked and saddened by Ross Craigthorn's death, and I want to take this occasion to appeal to all of the listeners my voice might be reaching. If any of you, anywhere, have information about this terrible crime, any knowledge of some enemy Ross Craigthorn might have had, something in his past life which might have caused his murder, I do wish you'd communicate with me immediately."

Skinny Simon joined in at this point. "That's right, listeners. In fact, as you regulars to all-night land know, we have a teletype system right here in our control room. Any telegrams sent to us are transmitted directly to it, and we can have them on the air within 30 minutes of the time

85

you send them. We cannot accept phone calls—but telegrams, yes! Anyone with information about the Craigthorn killing, please wire us at once! We'll be here all night. Now, just a pause for a brief commercial message, and we'll be back with you."

They cut away for sixty seconds and then started up again. The Craigthorn case was discussed briefly before shifting to other matters. Harry Fox could always be depended upon to fill them in with some amusing data, and he took his cue now, replying to Skinny's leading question. "Harry, you're only an associate member, but I understand that you know a good deal about the organization, and about the early days of mystery writing. I understand that Charles Dickens even played around with mysteries back in the last century. Is that true?"

Harry nodded, then apparently realized that the listeners could not see his nod. "That's right, Skinny. Dickens, of course, wrote *Bleak House*, which has elements of mystery and crime about it. And he was well into *The Mystery of Edwin Drood*, a genuine whodunit, at the time of his death. It's generally assumed that he was so interested in mysteries because of his close personal relationship with Wilkie Collins, author of *The Woman in White* and *The Moonstone*. That last, of course, was the first full-length detective novel in the English language. There had been a couple of previous ones in French, by Emile Gaboriau."

Skinny grunted. "Wilkie Collins—was he the same as Charles Collins? I remember there was a Charles Collins who sometimes collaborated with Dickens on short things."

"No. Charles Collins was actually Wilkie Collins's brother, and he was also a son-in-law of Dickens. So, as you can see, the two families were closely related through marriage."

Max Winters chimed in at this point. "I may be a minority voice, but I have an awful feeling that too much attention is paid to the glorious past of the detective story. I'm just interested in its glorious present myself. I'm interested in the money that publishers pay, and I'm interested in the reviews that my novels get. I think there are a great many like me in the field. We belong to MWA and we support its aims, but we don't go poring over dusty old volumes to trace the antecedents of the detective story. We're just interested in here and now—today—and maybe tomorrow."

Dick McMullen, the agent, was quick to support him. While he talked, he tapped a pencil against his cheek, a nervous habit that intrigued Barney. "You're absolutely right there, Max. For all practical purposes, the detective novel started in the nineteen-twenties with Christie and Hammett and VanDine, and later with Stout and Queen and Gardner. Anything earlier, even Arthur Conan Doyle's Sherlock Holmes, belongs, for all practical purposes, to another era."

"Now I don't know about that," Barney interrupted. "It may belong to another era, but that's an era we owe an awful lot to. Certainly Agatha Christie's Hercule Poirot owes much to Sherlock Holmes. The early stories even have a sort of Watson character. In the same manner, the early Ellery Queen novels owe an acknowledged debt to Philo Vance, though certainly Queen far surpassed Vance in every respect, both as a detective and as a character."

Barney's back was to the control booth as he talked. Occasionally he managed to sneak a glance at Susan Veldt and the other girls. As the conversation droned on, interrupted by regularly spaced commercials, he was not surprised to see Miss Sweeney and Betty Rafferty growing bored. By the time the program had ended its second hour, the two of them got up, said a few words to Susan and departed. He noticed Betty yawn as they went out the door.

At the next commercial break, he said to Skinny, "We lost a couple of the girls. They couldn't take the rough hours."

The host nodded. "That's why I rarely have women on this show. I had a lady doctor once who fell asleep—sound asleep—sitting in that very chair you're in."

They cut back with the program and the talk droned on for another hour. Skinny took a break around three to whisper, "The food should be here at three-thirty. Then we all knock off for a half-hour's eating. Chinese food tonight. It's coming up from a little restaurant downtown. Good stuff. Egg rolls, all the trimmings."

While the time passed faster than Barney had expected, he was still happy when the break came. Some sort of recorded segment was put on, and Susan came out to join them.

"Where's the food? I'm starved!"

A crew of Chinese, looking somehow like midnight fugitives from a tong war, entered bearing white delicatessen containers of food. Barney had to admit it was good, even though he didn't care for Chinese nourishment as a rule. There was much casual chatting and a relaxed air settled over the whole proceedings.

"No telegrams came in," Skinny said. "That's surprising. I thought we'd at least get a few cranks."

"Telegrams cost money," Susan reminded him. "I'll bet you got a lot of cranks when you had a phone in here."

"Did we ever! One after the other! I had no time for the program. I was forever answering the telephone. We cut that out quick enough."

But when the show resumed at four A.M., Barney made one more appeal for information. "If anyone knows anything at all about the terrible killing of Ross Craigthorn at the Biltmore on Friday night, I ask him to telegraph me here at the studio right now. It's extremely important and certainly you'll be well rewarded for your efforts."

Skinny nodded and gave him a broad smile. Maybe the promise of a reward would bring the information they sought—whatever that might be. At this point, Barney himself didn't know just what they were seeking.

They went on with the program, with Skinny managing to get in plugs for all their most recent books. The one dud of the show was proving to be Frank Jesset, who had contributed no more than three sentences during the course of the night. Barney would not have been surprised to see him sneak out during one of the commercials, but he stuck to it, chain-smoking cigarettes and trying not to look bored. At one point they tried to shift the conversation over to confession magazines, but even in that field he had nothing to offer.

It was twenty minutes to five when Susan suddenly signaled from the control room. Something was up. She tiptoed into the studio, thrusting a torn sheet of telegraph paper in front of Barney. The message was short and to the point. *May have information regarding Craigthorn killing. Contact me this address noon Monday.* It was signed *Irma Black*, and gave the address of a residential hotel on lower Fifth Avenue.

By the time the program ended with a somewhat limping finish at five o'clock, Barney was ready to go to Irma Black's address at once. The others crowded around, giving suggestions.

"She's not there," Max said. "If she was there, she'd have said to come now. She's not going to be there till noon."

"She's probably sleeping," Harry said. "Why don't you give her a call and find out."

Barney bit his lip. "I don't know. It could be nothing. I hate to go chasing down there at this hour if it is nothing. Let's hold off till noon. Then I'll tackle her alone."

"Alone?" Susan .Veldt asked. "You're forgetting me, buddy. I'm tagging right along with you. This is still my story."

"All right," Barney agreed.

"Should I pick you up at your apartment?"

"I'll meet you down there. Noon. On the dot."

"What's that number on Fifth Avenue again?"

Barney showed her and then stuffed the telegram into his pocket. The others were drifting out, and he rode down on the elevator with Dick McMullen and Skinny. "How'd you think it went?" Dick asked. "This is my first experience on one of these things."

Skinny shrugged his shoulders. "After five nights a week, they're all pretty much the same. I think it was a good show, though. We'll probably be repeating it in a few months and I'll let you fellows know. You can listen to it yourself and hear what it sounds like. Sometimes I like 'em with a little more pepper—a little more spice. We got our highest audience rating the night we had three prostitutes and a pimp on—but I suppose you can't do that every night. Once in a while we have to settle for mystery writers." He chuckled as he said it.

Then the elevator door came open. The building's

watchman glanced sleepily at them and nodded to Skinny. They went out onto Seventh Avenue, strolling toward Times Square. Dawn was just starting to break and Barney glanced over toward the East River. Somewhere the sun would be coming up. He looked for Susan, but she had gone already. Home, probably—to sleep, or type up her notes on the night's activities. That was the place for him too—home.

It had been a long day.

Chapter Twelve

SUSAN VELDT

Tired as she was, Susan stayed awake long enough to type five single-spaced pages. Then she stapled them together and stuck them into her purse for delivery to Rowe in the morning. The morning? It was already morning. She looked out through bleary eyes at the dawn as it struck the Central Park trees, listening for some sign that the animals were awake. But there were no lionesque roars as yet to greet the new day. Perhaps even animals were sleepy on Monday mornings.

She turned in, setting her clock for ten, knowing that she'd have to stop by the office before she met Barney at Irma Black's apartment. The whole thing was probably a wild goose chase. Anyone demented enough to listen to those all-night shows surely wouldn't draw the line at sending a nutty telegram. Barney's voice had probably sounded sexy to her on the radio, and she wanted to lure him into bed for a little noontime love making. Stranger things have happened.

Susan thought about it, then swore at herself for letting her mind wander in that direction. Barney in bed. Hadn't she had enough of that the night before? Hadn't she cured herself for all time? No Barney. No bed. Let the mysterious Irma Black have him. She dropped her head on the pillow and was asleep almost at once.

When she awoke with the buzzing alarm clock in her ears, she knew she must dress quickly. The clock was old and had gone off ten minutes late. Still, she made it down to the *Manhattan* offices before eleven-thirty.

Her luck did not hold all the way, though. Arthur Rowe was just going into a staff meeting—the regular Monday morning session to plan next week's issue.

"I'll leave the notes in your box," she said.

"Good, good. We've got proofs on this week's issue if you want to see it. My secretary has them."

It was a bit of an editorial courtesy that he allowed his writers to see proofs of an issue, even of the parts that they had not written themselves. She glanced over them with interest, noting that he had managed to get in a stop-press notice of Craigthorn's killing, with promise of a detailed series to follow. It made her feel good. It made her feel that she hadn't stayed up all night and typed for an hour in vain. She glanced through the morning mail, saw nothing of interest, and then caught a cab for lower Fifth Avenue.

When she arrived, she saw that Barney was already there, pacing the sidewalk and glancing at his watch. "You're late," he said, "but I suppose that's not surprising."

"I had to stop by the office."

"I know. You explained your work habits to me. Come on. It's after twelve."

The woman named Irma Black answered their second ring. Her features surprised Susan, almost as much as her apparent age. She was no sexy young wanton trying to lure Barney Hamet anywhere. She looked fifty or more, though a hard life could have added lines to an already sagging face and dumpy frame. Her flowered dress hung on her like a sack, and she seemed to be wearing no makeup.

She led them into the small furnished apartment. "I was listening to the radio. I missed the beginning, but I caught the part where you asked for help, Mr. Hamet. You *are* Mr. Hamet, aren't you?"

"That's correct," Barney said.

"Who's this you've brought with you?"

"Miss Veldt. She's assisting me."

"No police. This isn't a police thing, is it?"

"No police," Barney assured her. "The police come later, after we get something. Do you have something to give us?"

"You mentioned money on the program."

"I don't think I specifically mentioned money. I might have said that any information would be rewarded."

"Well, isn't it the same thing? Isn't a reward money?"

"Perhaps I was thinking of a reward in heaven."

Irma Black snorted. "I take what I get on this earth. Let someone else worry about heaven."

"Do you know Ross Craigthorn? Did you know him?"

"Of course I knew him. Boy, did I know Ross Craigthorn!"

"Do you want to tell me about it?"

"Not until I see the color of your money."

Barney was growing impatient. "Look, either you know something or you don't. I'm surely not going to pay off money for nothing. What sort of information do you have?"

"I know about Ross Craigthorn in his youth. Way, way back. Out in the midwest in a little town called June."

"June?"

"That's right. Like the month. June, Nebraska. Nice place."

"That's where you're from?"

"That's where we're all from. Ross Craigthorn, and me, and the other one."

"What other one?" Barney asked.

"Ha! That would be telling, wouldn't it? Ross was a wild boy in his youth. He and this other one—they did bad things. They did a bad thing to me."

"What sort of a bad thing? You can speak up clearer than that. We're all adults here."

But Irma Black shook her head. "Took me a long time to track him down. Even after I started seeing him on television I wasn't sure it was the same person. His name was a little different in those days—not much, though. The 'Craig' was still there, and that made me think it was him. I knew he'd come to New York. I think they both went to

93

New York after it happened."

"What happened?"

"I'm telling it! It's my story! I'm telling it! I've lived with it—and I'm telling it!" Her hands fluttered with excitement.

"All right. Tell it, then." Susan was making unobtrusive shorthand notes, and she hoped this wouldn't scare the old woman.

"They both came to New York, or at least Ross did. I don't know for sure where the other one went. Ross told me he was successful, though. Both of them successful. Money. I came here to get money from them, I suppose."

"Would you call it blackmail?"

"No. Just getting what's due me after all these years. For what they did to me."

"Tell us about it," Barney urged again. It was hot in the apartment, hot for April, and Susan wished that the woman would open a window. She wondered how Barney could stand the heat.

"Money," the woman said again. "I don't tell nothing till I see some money."

Barney sighed and started pacing the floor. "How much?"

"Well, I was going to get a hundred thousand dollars from Ross Craigthorn."

"A hundred . . . why, that's ridiculous! He never would have given you that much."

She smiled her knowing smile. "Ross Craigthorn was a rich man. A hundred thousand would have been nothing to him. He probably makes that in a week."

"You've been reading the wrong fan magazines, I'm afraid," Barney told her. "A hundred thousand dollars would probably be six months' income to Craigthorn—after taxes. Whatever your hold over him, I don't think he would have paid that much to keep his past a secret."

She stared uncertainly, biting her lower lip. To Susan, she looked like nothing so much as an old hag, a witch from some half-forgotten childhood fairy tale. Perhaps the witch in Snow White with the poisoned apple. Mirror, mirror, on the wall . . .

"Besides," Barney reminded her, "Ross Craigthorn is

94

dead. If there ever was a hundred thousand, it's not there anymore. Let's talk sensibly."

"Fifty thousand?" she asked, uncertainly. "I came all the way to New York from June."

"No fifty thousand."

Susan could almost imagine him calculating the amount of money in the MWA treasury. From what she knew of the organization, it couldn't be much. Maybe a few thousand dollars, at best.

"I could maybe give you five hundred," Barney said.

"Don't even talk to me. Go away. I'll find the other one and get the hundred thousand out of him. Ross said he was famous too. I'll find him."

"Famous doesn't mean rich. Take the five hundred and be happy you've got it."

"Go back and talk to your friends. You can do better than that," she said. "A lot better than five hundred measly dollars after I came halfway across the country."

"What you were doing was blackmailing Ross Craigthorn. That's a crime. I could have you arrested right now for it."

"No blackmailing. You'd have to prove that."

"You wrote to him? Contacted him in some way?"

"That's for me to know," she said. "I have to go out now. You just go see your people and find out how much money you can raise, and then you come back and see me—tonight. If the money is enough, I talk. Otherwise, you're out of luck."

Susan saw Barney shrug his shoulders. "All right," he said. "I guess there's nothing else I can do. Come on, Susan. We'll be back later."

They left her in the apartment, and heard her bolt her door behind them. Barney did not talk until they reached the street, and then he said, "I don't know. Maybe she's got something, and maybe she hasn't. The whole thing might be a big bluff."

"Do you think she killed Craigthorn?"

"I don't see why. She wouldn't kill her meal ticket. Not if she thought he was going to cough up a hundred thousand. She said there were two of them. The other is the one we have to find. The partner in Craigthorn's past."

"And where do we look for him?"

Barney stared up at the sky. There were a few clouds, but the sun was showing through. "She's our only link to any of it. We have to work through her, and I guess that means I've got to find some money, or at least the promise of some money, and come back to talk to her again. Let's get a cab and go uptown."

Chapter Thirteen

VICTOR JONES

He saw them leaving the apartment building just as he arrived across the street—Barney Hamet and Susan Veldt. They'd already seen her, then, and who knows what she might have told them?

Victor Jones watched while they stood for a moment on the curb talking, and then hailed a cab. Fifth Avenue was one-way southbound, and he kept his eye on the taxi to see in what direction they would be headed. They took the next right and he guessed that meant they were heading back uptown, perhaps to MWA headquarters, by way of Sixth Avenue.

He lit a cigarette and stood in the doorway, contemplating the building across the street. It was just after one o'clock, and even down here in the Village there was a certain amount of noontime traffic. He waited until the light changed—then he came out of his doorway and walked quickly across the street, into the apartment building the two had just left.

She hadn't even bothered to register under an assumed name, and it was easy to find her place. Easy—especially when he stepped onto the landing and saw her just coming out her door. "Mrs. Black! Mrs. Black! Wait a moment!" he said.

She turned and looked, not recognizing him. "Who . . . I was just going out."

"Can I have just a word with you for a moment? It's very important."

"I was just going out," she repeated.

"It's about money," he said.

"Well . . ."

"A great deal of money. One hundred thousand dollars."

"Who are you?" But the talk of money had persuaded her. She stepped aside and let him enter the apartment, then closed and bolted the door behind them. "Who are you?" she asked again.

"I'm a man who's come to talk to you about money, Mrs. Black."

"Are you a friend of Ross Craigthorn's? That was the money he was going to give me. A hundred thousand dollars."

"Was he going to give it to you? Was he, Irma?"

Then she recognized him. Her hand flew to her mouth and her eyes seemed to bore through his head. "*You!*" she said. "Victor Jones! After all these years . . . *you!*"

"How are you, Irma? How's the world been treating you?"

"How am I? I'm the same as you. The same as Ross. We're three of a kind, I guess. God! That was a long time ago! Twenty . . . how many years? Twenty-two years? It was after the war, wasn't it? I never thought I'd see you again. Ross was easy to find because he was on television every night. I saw him and I remembered that face. Remembered how he bent over me that night. You were the one, though. You, Victor. I never thought I'd see you again to my dying day."

"So now we're here—the two of us. Just like old times, isn't it, Irma?"

"Not like old times. Ross was around in the old times. There were three of us. Three of us . . . three kids."

"We were in our twenties. We weren't kids."

"We were kids. God! Remember how it was? That week? Seven days! Remember, we went back over the state line to June? Just the three of us. Ah . . . that was a time! Victor . . . you and Ross and me. That was a time!"

"It surely was, Irma. What brings you east?"

"Well, I saw Ross on television. I'm a poor woman. I'm almost fifty now. What was I to do? I needed money. I was married for a while, but it didn't work out, and then my husband died. What would work out after the week I spent with you, Victor? I came east because I needed money. I was never one to live off welfare. Us midwesterners are a hardy breed, you know."

Victor Jones nodded. "Hardy."

"I came to New York and I contacted Ross. I told him what I needed. I didn't think there'd be any problem. He was a little reluctant, though. Called it blackmail. Blackmail! An awful word! Awful! He said I was well named. Irma Black for blackmail. But things aren't black or white in this world any more, are they, Victor? You know that better than anyone else."

"I know it, Irma." -

"Oh, if only I could be back there again! We have to grow old, and that's the awful part of it—the awful part of everything. We grow old, and the old friends change. The old times fade. All we have are our memories. The present is never quite as good as the past, is it? And nobody even thinks about the future."

"Some people think about it, Irma. Ross thought about it. That's why he didn't give you the money."

"Oh, he would have given it to me. He talked a lot, but he didn't want to ruin his career. He had some wild idea about going to his public, telling them all that happened. He said the statute of limitations had run out and they couldn't arrest him for anything. But arrest isn't the point, it is, Victor? He was someone in the public eye. If this ever came out, he would just be ruined. When I think of the number of laws you two broke in that week . . ."

"Irma . . ."

"I bet you never expected to see me again, did you?"

"No. I guess I never did. You were someone from the past, and I think at times I simply forgot about your existence."

"You were the one. You were the leader of the whole

thing. Ross, he was a follower in those days. I was sort of surprised that he got where he did because he was really a follower. You were the leader."

"I suppose I was," Victor Jones said. "Will you be going back to June now?"

"Of course. As soon as you give me the hundred thousand dollars that Ross promised. He's dead now, you know. Dead. Somebody killed him."

"Why would anyone do that?"

"I can't imagine. Communists, I suppose. Sometimes I'd listen to his program and you know, he was death on communists. I suppose there was a communist, and he shot Ross. Now you'll just have to give me the money."

"Oh, I couldn't do that. Besides," Victor said, with a slight smile, "you don't even know who I am. I can walk out of this apartment and vanish into seven or eight million people out there in the street. I'm nobody to you. I'm not on television every night of the week."

Imra Black sighed. "Ross said you were famous—or rich—I forget which he said now. But you're well known, anyway."

"New York is full of well-known people. I sometimes think everyone in New York is well known, in his own special way." Victor Jones took out another cigarette. "So that proves nothing, you see?"

"Ah . . . but you're forgetting I know what you look like now. And you don't really look that much different from the old days, now that I see you in better light. There might even be some pictures around that I could dig up—pictures that Ross's uncle took. He was always talking about his uncle taking pictures—all that week we were together. And the uncle's still alive and kicking! It would be difficult, but I could find a reporter on one of these newspapers, one of these tabloid scandal sheets. He'd probably give me some money for my story. And I'd tell it, and I'd say that somewhere in New York this famous man . . ."

"Not famous, Irma. Hardly famous."

"Well, this rich man, then, or whatever. You're dressed well. I can see you're not poor. Anyway, I'd tell him, and he'd print the story and the pictures, and the police would be interested, of course, wouldn't they? Wouldn't they, Victor? Because the statute of limitations might have applied in Ross's case, but certainly not in yours. In that state, the statute of limitations doesn't apply to kidnapping, Victor. And that's what you did—you kidnapped me, all alone by yourself. Besides, the police might even think you killed poor Ross."

"Why would they get that idea?"

"I don't know. They'd be looking into all his old friends and connections. They'd find out what happened back there twenty-two years ago. There wouldn't be any fingerprints, but they might be able to track you down in some other way. Maybe there would be fingerprints, though. Maybe you left some at the scene. Did you ever think of that?"

"There were no fingerprints," Victor Jones said. "What do you want, Irma?"

"I told you. Money. Money enough so that I can live for the rest of my days without ever having to worry. Without having to pick up men in third-rate bars or marry a guy I didn't love. Or stand in line at the welfare office. Money enough so that I wouldn't have to do any of these things. That's what I want, Victor. That's what I've always wanted. I'd like to travel—maybe down to Mexico, or even over to Europe. Travel is broadening, they say. I'm getting old, Victor. We all are. I'm almost too old for anything now. It's so important to me to have security in my old age. And if there's anybody who owes it to me, it's you and Ross. The two of you. And he's dead."

"I can give you a little money, Irma," Victor said, reaching into his pocket. He took out a wallet and pulled some bills from it. "Enough for your plane fare back to June."

"Not a little money. Now now, Victor. Big money! The man that was here before—he's going to come back tonight."

"What man is that?"

"A man. I don't know. He was on the radio last night. I heard him, and I sent him a telegram. I'll sell my information to the highest bidder, Victor. I have no great loyalties to you anymore. It was a week of fun back in those days so many years ago, but now I'm getting old."

He stood up and walked over to her chair. "Irma, Irma . . . you couldn't blackmail me."

She looked up into his eyes, and perhaps that was when she saw it, when she realized there was something just a bit frightening about the expression on his face. "I really think you did kill Ross! I was only joking about it before, but . . . but I think you did! It's in your eyes, isn't it? You could kill! You could kill to keep your past a secret! And you killed Ross Craigthorn, didn't you?"

Victor Jones did not answer.

"Didn't you? Didn't you?"

Her small fists were beating at his chest, reminding him. It might have been twenty-two years ago, and there she was in his arms once more. There she was. Reminding him that the emotions of love and death are not really that far apart. Life began, and life ended . . . sometimes, it ended just like this.

"Ahh . . . Irma . . . Irma," he said, and slipped his hands up to her throat.

"No!"

She broke away, squirming, agile now as a tiger—trying for what? The door? No. The telephone. Trying for the telephone.

But he was on her in an instant, grabbing the instrument from her hand. He gave her a glancing blow with it, and she fell back stunned.

And opened her mouth to scream.

He jumped on her, wrapping the telephone cord, in two quick motions, around her throat—pulling, tugging, choking off the scream before it could grow in volume.

"*Victor . . .*"

But it was a sigh rather than a scream.

"Victor . . ."

A sigh that died to a whisper, died to nothing.

He pulled the cord tight, looping it one more time, and kept on tugging. She may have said his name again, but he was not certain. It could have been only in his memory.

His memory of twenty-two years ago, when he'd held her in his arms for the first time.

Chapter Fourteen

BARNEY HAMET

Barney spent much of the late afternoon in Harry Fox's office, relating the events of the day. He trusted Harry, and so he told him about the visit to Irma Black and her demand for money.

Harry shrugged his shoulders and tapped his fingertips together. "I sure don't think MWA is going to come up with a big chunk of money, Barney. They just don't have it. You know better than I how much money's in the till, but anything more than a few hundred would pretty much exhaust the treasury, I'd think. Why don't you just take the police down there and scare her a bit?"

"I might have to do that," Barney agreed. "I might have to do it soon, before she gets scared on her own, and leaves town."

"Do you think she's really got something?"

"I don't know," he replied. And he didn't know. Of course Irma Black, with all her knowledge might still have no direct connection with the murder at the Biltmore. But she certainly seemed worth following through at this point.

Harry Fox scratched his balding head, rummaged around his desk until he found a cigarette in a half-empty pack. "All right," he said. "So maybe she has something. I suppose it's worth your while talking to her again. Look—I have some money I can advance for this thing. Find out how much she needs. If you want, I'll go down and talk to her with you."

Barney thought about that. "We'll never be able to meet her price. I think it might be wiser to call that detective fellow, George. He might just be able to throw a scare into her."

Fox shrugged. "Do what you want. You know best, Barney."

"I think it's worth a try. Maybe George can scare her a bit. At least it's better than the dead end we're at now."

He walked to the window and looked out at the traffic below. The afternoon shadows were already lengthening, and though the temperature had warmed a bit, most people wore topcoats.

"So tell me about yourself. What have you been doing, Harry?"

"The usual, Barney, the usual. Trying to make a living. I was dead this morning after being up all night on Skinny's show, I'll tell you that!"

"How'd you think it went?"

"Could have been better, I guess. We didn't really grapple with anything. That's the trouble with those all-night sessions. We got in our little plugs, and we talked a bit about mysteries, and you had your appeal for help in the case, but we never really came to grips with the thing. I'd like to have a whole night spent some time talking about the more physical aspects of a murder. About intricate plot devices—that sort of thing. You know—I think they could do a whole program just on locked rooms, or unusual murder methods, or ways of disposing of a body."

Barney nodded, turning from the window. "Somebody, I think it was Basil Davenport, a few years ago, edited a couple of anthologies, and pretty good ones, too. One was on unusual murder methods. The other was on ways to dispose of a body. I think he pretty much covered them."

Harry Fox nodded. "I know the books, but there are a few he missed. Here, I'll give you a free idea, Barney. Maybe you can use it in a novel and dedicate the book to me or something. This is one of those things that proves that truth is a bit stranger than fiction. Stranger, and more disagreeable, I guess. Remember the OAS? The secret army in France? Dedicated to keeping Algeria as a part of France? They were active in the late fifties and early sixties, before de Gaulle clamped down on them. They had a few tricks. There was one especially, for disposing of a body, that I've never seen used in fiction."

"What was that?" Barney asked, settling down to be interested. This sort of talk always intrigued him. And he knew that Harry Fox was a walking encyclopedia on matters criminous.

"Well, they'd kill a guy—shoot him in the head, usually—take all his clothes, anything else that might identify him, and then bind the body very tightly in chicken wire. Then they'd take it out into the ocean on a small boat and they'd dump it overboard. It seems that as the body decomposed and became bloated by sea water, the flesh was shredded by the chicken wire—which, of course, would not yield to the pressure of the expanding skin. This shredding of the flesh, in turn, attracted swarms of fish. They went to work on the pieces and devoured enough of it so that what little was left was completely unidentifiable. No worry about weighting the body down, and would it come to the surface or wouldn't it. By the time anything was found, it was so shredded, so eaten by fish, so decomposed by the sea, that there was nothing left for anyone to identify. It was a fairly ingenious system, I suppose—if you don't get sick to your stomach thinking about it."

"What magazine am I supposed to sell a story like that to? *The Ladies' Home Journal*?"

"I just give you the ideas, Barney. You figure out what to do with them."

"Thanks. Thanks, Harry. You're a sport. If I ever write it, I'll dedicate it to you. Maybe it'll even win an Edgar."

Harry Fox was beginning to straighten his desk. It was almost quitting time. "Know something, Barney? Those Edgars might almost have been called Henrys."

"Henrys?"

He nodded. "For Henry Fielding, the author of *Tom Jones*."

"Oh, come on, Harry!"

But the little man only smiled at Barney's exasperation. "Really, I wouldn't kid you! Fielding was a lawyer, and later became a magistrate. Around 1748, he was named Justice of the Peace for Westminster and Middlesex, and after that he wrote some brief pamphlets on crime and criminals. As a magistrate, he was so successful that he practically cleared crime out of one of London's worst districts. More important to our discussion, he established—with the help of his half-brother, Sir John Fielding—England's first efficient plainclothes detective force, the predecessor of the famed Bow Street Runners and of Scotland Yard's Criminal Investigation Department. Fielding's last novel, *Amelia*, reflected this growing interest in social problems. It's altogether possible that if ill health and an early death at the age of forty-seven hadn't cut short his career he would have gone on to write the world's first detective story."

"And we'd have Henrys instead of Edgars," Barney agreed. "Harry—sometimes I think you know more about eighteenth and nineteenth century literature than anyone in New York."

"I know a bit," Harry Fox agreed modestly.

"Closing up shop now? How about going for a drink?"

"Don't you want to get back down to Mrs. Black?"

Barney nodded in agreement. "I should. Let me use your phone to call police headquarters. I want to see if I can catch Detective George."

George was in. He answered the phone almost immediately, in a bored voice that grew only slightly interested when Barney identified himself. After listening in silence to the purpose of the call, he finally said, "Don't you think you're about twelve hours late notifying me? Don't you think you should have called me as soon as that telegram came in to your foolish radio program? The woman could be halfway back to Nebraska by now. Or she could be dead, for all you know or care."

"Look, I called you, didn't I? I'm cutting you in. Now, do you want to meet me down there, or don't you?"

106

"What's the address?" George asked.

Barney gave it to him, then said goodbye to Harry Fox and headed out to get a cab. He never drove his own car around the city when he could avoid it, and right now, in the late afternoon, he figured that the cab trip down there would be tough enough. He was not far wrong. Inching downtown at ten miles an hour, he was not at all surprised to see a police car pulled up in front of the address when he arrived. He was a bit surprised, however, when a second car arrived on the scene almost at once, with its siren blaring. He wondered what George was up to.

The detective was standing at the top of the stairs, waiting for him, outside of Irma Black's apartment. "You mystery writer guys—you really know how to handle things, don't you?"

"What do you mean?" Barney asked, but he already could feel a chill on his spine. Something was wrong. Something had happened, something bad.

"I mean that this Black woman is dead. You wanna come in and take a look at her? Identify her?"

"Dead?"

"Strangled with a telephone cord. He almost twisted her head right off her body."

Barney stepped through the doorway, fighting down a growing nausea in the pit of his stomach. Yes, she was there, sprawled on the floor, entangled in the telephone.

"This is the woman you talked to?" George asked.

"That's her. Irma Black. From June, Nebraska." He'd have to look at a map sometime and see where June was—see what kind of a town it was, what kind of a place she wouldn't be going back to now.

"Any idea who did it?" George asked.

"No idea, unless you want a wild guess. It could have been the same person that killed Ross Craigthorn. There were two of them connected with Irma Black somehow in her past, back in the Midwest. She told me that much. Wouldn't tell me more unless she got some money. Like I explained to you on the phone, I thought maybe we could throw a scare into her."

"You threw a scare into somebody. The murderer. Who

107

knew she was here? Who knew you came to see her? Were you alone?"

"That girl, Susan Veldt, was with me."

Barney ran a hand across his eyes, suddenly very tired.

"Nobody reported the telephone out of order?"

"You write too many stories," George told him. "Telephones get left off the hook maybe a million times a day in this city. Nobody reports anything."

Other police were arriving now—photographers, someone from the medical examiner's office, fingerprint men, men in business suits with badges pinned incongruously to the outside of their jackets. They joked a bit as they went about their work.

"She's dead all right," one of them said, straightening up from the body.

"How long?" Detective George asked.

"A few hours. Hard to say exactly. We'll leave that for the autopsy."

"You left her at what time, Mr. Hamet?"

Barney tried to think. It wasn't every day he saw a body, even when he was writing about them. They were things of black and white, paper and typewriter ribbon. Not flesh and blood like this. Now, in the space of seventy-two hours, he'd been confronted with two of them. Two of them, brutally murdered—perhaps by someone he knew very well.

"We were here from maybe a bit after twelve till around one. She said she had to go out then."

"Did she go out?"

"I don't know. Susan and I left. We didn't see anyone lurking about."

"Who else knew you were coming here?"

Barney explained again about the radio program. "I suppose everyone in the studio knew about it. When the telegram came in, we all looked at it. After the show, we debated about it a bit. Some of them wanted me to come right down, but I figured I'd better wait till noon."

"Sure, wait till noon. Wait a few days, why don't you? Give the murderer plenty of chance! You writers!" The detective turned away in disgust.

"How did I know she'd get killed? There were five of us

on the program. Am I supposed to figure one of them did it?"

"I wouldn't be a bad figure. They had the address. And it sounds to me as if they might have had a motive, if one of them killed Craigthorn. Give me their names."

Barney sighed, feeling somehow on the brink of a great betrayal. "Well, there's Harry Fox . . . you've got all these names!"

"Give 'em to me again."

"All right. Harry Fox. You know him. You met him the other night. Max Winters, you know. You were questioning him at his hotel. Dick McMullen, the agent, Frank Jesset. Jesset's the one who was a friend of Craigthorn's."

"I know. Frank Jesset."

But Barney noticed the flicker of interest in the detective's eyes. There was something more to Jesset, and the police knew about it, whatever it was.

"And myself. We were the five on the panel. There was the guy in the control room. I don't know if you want to investigate him or not. And there was Susan Veldt. She was in the control room too. And a couple of other girls— Betty Rafferty from the office, and this Miss Sweeney, Craigthorn's secretary. She came with Jesset, but she didn't stay long. She and Betty went home after a couple of hours. It's a long stretch, staying up all night like that."

"Who else?"

"No one at all. That's it."

Detective George closed his eyes for a moment against the popping of a flash bulb. "All right. Whose show was it?"

"Well, Skinny Simon's. Of course he was there. Didn't I mention him?"

"No, you didn't."

"All right, Skinny Simon. I thought you knew whose show it was."

"So that makes a few more than six people. That makes . . . five panelists, and Skinny, and the engineer, and three women."

"Oh, come on! You'll have the whole city of New York on your suspect list before long."

"How many of these people were at the dinner Friday night?"

"Well, all of us on the panel were, and all the women."

"Was Skinny at the dinner?"

"Sure, he was there. We were talking about the show that night."

"Okay," the detective said. "Where were you this afternoon after you and Susan Veldt left here?"

"Where was I? Well, part of the time I was up at Harry Fox's office, till I called you. Why? Are you suspecting me of this thing now?"

George gave a customary shrug. His suit was as rumpled as ever, and his hair had the same wild look, even though it was not windy out today. "Look, you called me to come down here with you, to find the body with you. It's exactly the sort of thing a murderer would do. I know, because I read it in a detective story once."

"All right, call Harry Fox. He'll tell you I was with him."

"Were you with him all the time? All afternoon? Since you left this apartment?"

"Not all the time. I took Susan uptown and we had lunch. It was probably two-thirty or three before I went up to Harry's. Then I was with him the rest of the afternoon, till now."

"All right," the detective said. "Stay available."

Someone else appeared—a lieutenant, apparently, and spoke a few words to George. "You're out of your precinct, boy."

"Yeah, I know," Detective George said. "Downtown, slumming. This might tie in with the Craigthorn killing Friday night up at the Biltmore, and that *is* my precinct. Do what you can, and get me a report on it, huh?"

"All right," the man said, slightly appeased.

"Can I go now?" Barney asked.

"Yeah, I guess there's nothing much for you here. You can go. We'll be in touch."

Barney went downstairs, started up to MWA headquarters, and then for no reason at all paused at a pay phone long enough to call Susan Veldt at her office. But it was after five, and they told him she had left for the day.

110

Chapter Fifteen

SUSAN VELDT

On Tuesday morning, as she was leaving her daily rough draft of the article in Arthur Rowe's file basket, Susan heard his secretary call to her. "Mr. Rowe wants to see you. He asked you to wait in his office until he's free."

"All right," she said.

She knew very little about the murder of Irma Black. Only what she'd heard on the late news, and read in the morning *Times*. They hadn't played up the story too much, apparently not yet connecting it with the Craigthorn killing. She'd been unable to reach Barney, and so she knew no other details. But in her own mind she saw the makings of a fabulous story. She wished for perhaps the first time in her life that she worked on a daily newspaper—that she didn't have to wait for a weekly deadline to roll around, then wait several more days to see her story in print. *Manhattan* was great for reviews and features, but it was hell on spot news.

Arthur Rowe entered in his shirt sleeves, looking somehow disheveled. She wasn't really used to seeing him like this, and the sight startled her for a moment.

"All right," he said. "Give me what you've got."

"What I've got is next to nothing. You read in the paper about this woman, this Irma Black?"

He nodded.

"She's the one that sent the telegram to the program."

"Did you go down there yesterday with him?" He picked her notes out of his *In* basket.

"That's my rough draft. Read it and weep. As near as I can tell, we were there about an hour before the murder."

"Great." He slumped in his chair. "Look, we're on to something big. I don't want you to blow it. This can be the making of the magazine. With you on the inside track, we just might beat Mr. Barney Hamet to the solution, even."

"I don't know about that," she said. "I'm no detective."

"Just don't get involved with the guy. I don't want any emotional business standing in the way."

His words made her think back to the Saturday night encounter. It might seem funny some day, but just now she wasn't in the mood for fun. She found, to her own amazement, a pang of discomfort as she remembered what she had done to Barney Hamet. Why had she done it? Did she fear all men that much?

"Don't worry. I'm not getting emotionally involved with him. He's just another guy, and I've had plenty in my life."

Rowe lit his pipe, drew on it, took it from his mouth, and studied it for a moment. "Clogged again. These new pipes are never any good until they're broken in."

"I'll buy you an old one for Christmas."

"Thanks." He puffed. "So what's next on the agenda for the boy detective?"

"I don't really know," she answered honestly. "I suppose the police are questioning him about this latest thing, trying to tie it in with the first killing. They'll probably come around to see me, too."

"I'll try to hold the deadline as long as I can for you. See if you can get enough to make a really meaty article."

She nodded in agreement, then rose to go back to her desk. There was the usual office routine to be attended to—letters from a few disgruntled readers about her earlier articles, including an especially bitter one from someone connected with the Tony Awards. Apparently they did not go for her flip style, and they were ready to tell her so. They were objecting to a preliminary story in the last issue, since her full story on the Tony Awards wouldn't be out till the following day.

She went back to her apartment after work, and found a message there to call Barney Hamet. She looked up his phone number in the book and called his apartment.

"I got your message," she said. "What's up?"

He sounded tired, and she gathered he'd been having another long session with the police. "How would you like to go on a little trip with me?"

"Business or pleasure?"

"This would be all business. Sorry."

"Where to?"

"A place called June, Nebraska."

"June? Where that woman was from! Of course! You think you might find something in her background!"

"I don't know what I might find, but it seems to be worth a try. It's the sort of thing we could probably do better than the regular police. I'm not taking you along to give *Manhattan* any news beat on the story, either. I simply need a research assistant. There might be a lot of digging through old newspapers, talking to people around the town. I need another pair of feet to cover all the territory. Are you in?"

"I'm in," she said. "Just try and keep me out!"

Chapter Sixteen

BARNEY HAMET

After he talked to Susan Veldt on the phone, Barney scrambled an egg and fried some bacon for supper. He was a perennial breakfast eater, and when he was alone, he'd eat breakfast three times a day. It was his favorite meal—much preferable to the somewhat exotic foods offered in most of New York's restaurants. He never imagined himself as much of an eater, despite the fact that his broad shoulders and bulky appearance gave him the appearance of being a bit overweight. Maybe it was just that he ate the wrong food. Or maybe breakfast three times a day could be fattening.

He was just finishing it when the downstairs buzzer sounded, and he walked to the intercom system. "Yes. Who's there?"

Far below, someone cleared his throat. "This is Frank Jesset. I was on the program with you Sunday night. I'd like a few words with you, if you're free."

"Sure," Barney said. "Come on up."

"Miss Sweeney is with me."

"Miss . . . oh, yes! Certainly. Bring her along."

Well, Barney mused, Frank Jesset and Miss Sweeney. Ross Craigthorn's closest friend. Perhaps in the privacy of Barney's apartment, Jesset would prove more talkative than he had on Sunday night's radio show.

The two came hurriedly, as if they were collecting for the Red Cross, glancing nervously about the room, taking in Barney's books and his typewriter and the few remaining mementos of his married life.

It was Miss Sweeney who spoke first, her dark head bobbing. "You seem to be getting further on this case than the police. We thought we should have a talk with you."

"Thanks for the compliment, but I'm not doing anything they wouldn't do."

"You're finding bodies," Jesset said. "This woman, Irma Black . . ."

"Yes," Barney admitted cautiously.

"Miss Sweeney here has some information . . ."

"Wait a minute," Barney interrupted. "Perhaps we should be on a first-name basis. Miss Sweeney, I'm sure you have some very sweet, sincere, first name we could use."

She blinked her eyelashes at him and hardened the line of her lips. "My name is Mary, and I don't much like it. If you want to use it, you can, but I prefer to be called Miss Sweeney."

Barney shrugged. "All right, Miss Sweeney. You have some information?"

"I was telling it," Jesset said, with growing belligerence. "She has some information. It might help, it might not. But we don't want to get further involved with the police. We're involved deeply enough now. Do you know that they actually suspect us of having something to do with that murder? With that awful crime? That's right! One detective even hinted that the two of us were . . . well . . . having an affair!"

"I can't imagine that," Barney said, with a touch of irony.

"Whatever our personal relationship is, it has nothing to do with Ross Craigthorn, or with his murder. Miss Sweeney was his secretary. I was a close friend. That's it. We've come to give you this information. Do you want it? If you don't want it, then I'm sure the police will."

"I want any information I can get," Barney said. "It's

about this Irma Black?"

"That's right." Miss Sweeney took over the story at this point. "A few weeks ago, Ross Craigthorn received a letter. It was marked personal, but, of course, I still saw the return address. And I remembered. Irma Black. It had an address someplace in the Midwest."

"Nebraska?" Barney prodded. "A town called June, Nebraska?"

"That's it! I knew it was a funny name! A name that I hadn't heard before, but that I should remember because it was so uncommon. June, Nebraska. The letter was postmarked from New York, though. I got the impression she might just have moved to New York and didn't have a permanent return address here yet."

"I guess that was the case," Barney said. "Do you think you could find this letter? Is it still among Ross Craigthorn's papers?"

"I don't know," she answered, playing coy.

"Come on! Come on! You didn't come here for nothing. You didn't come here just to tell me about a letter you saw in an envelope three weeks ago. You've gone through his papers, and you have the letter, and you brought it to show me. Let's get on with this business and cut out beating around the bush."

She shot a glance at Frank Jesset, then shrugged and reached into her handbag. "You realize, of course, this is not exactly the perfect secretary's function. Amalgamated Broadcasting would fire me if they ever knew I took this from his desk."

"I could argue, Miss Sweeney, that it *is* the perfect secretary's function to try and discover the murderer of her employer. Anything you do, I'm sure, would be appreciated by Ross Craigthorn." He took the letter and unfolded it.

Dear Ross,

Excuse the informality, but I do feel that I know you quite well, even after twenty-two years.

I have seen you on television, and of course, I recognized you after a while. You didn't change your name all that

116

much—Craig to Craigthorn. I sort of like the Craigthorn. It makes you sound wealthy, like somone in government service maybe.

Ross, I'm writing you because I've been ill. My husband died and my life is at loose ends. I feel that I need some money to make a fresh start. There are two of you I could turn to. You and Victor. But I have not yet been able to locate Victor. I assume he is in New York, and perhaps in time I could find him.

But I have come to the city and taken an apartment mainly in the hope of talking with you. Even in the old days you were always the better of the two. Better. Maybe that's not the right word. I suppose Victor was always the better of the two. But you were the more sympathetic. You were kinder.

I don't want to do anything that's going to harm you in any way, Ross, but I know I must have money. And so I've come to you. You're a wealthy man. I read somewhere in the newspaper that you make more than a quarter of a million dollars a year, with your television show and other interests.

I don't want that much, because I realize you have other responsibilities. Say, a hundred thousand dollars. Enough money to keep me for the rest of my days, Ross. And it would hardly be missed by you.

Could you see your way clear to do that for me, Ross? One last gesture for those old days? For that week we spent together? Could you? This is in no way a threat, but I must say, of course, that if I do not receive any money from you, or from Victor, that I would have to look for it in other ways.

One way would be to sell the newspapers an account of that week in detail. And what detail! Remembered by a middle-aged woman—a frustrated middle-aged woman, Ross.

Yes, I can remember all the details, and I can make them really sing. I could tell them all about Caesar and Raven, and how it was, back then.

I'm not certain of my address yet, but I'll be contacting you. I'll phone you within the next day or two to hear your decision. I hope that it will be favorable for both our sakes.

The letter was signed—*Love*, with a little scrawly question mark after it, and then, *Irma Black*.

Barney read it over a second time, trying to puzzle it out. There was much meat to it, confirming what he already suspected. And one thing hopped out at him, more than any other. *Caesar and Raven*. He remembered the shattered Raven at the MWA dinner. Ross had been trying to tell him something. The Raven. Raven.

"Was there any other correspondence?" he asked Miss Sweeney. "Any phone calls?"

"I don't know about that. Mr. Craigthorn always got a number of phone calls in the course of a day, many from unidentified women. The newscasting business is like that. I tried to screen them as best I could, but quite often some crank callers got through to him. I don't remember anyone identifying herself as Irma Black, but that doesn't mean she didn't call."

"I think you'll agree," Jesset interrupted, "that this letter clears Miss Sweeney and myself of any complicity in the crime. Obviously this thing has its roots in the past."

Barney Hamet blinked and leaned back in his chair. "Well, that's what we're led to believe. As a mystery writer, of course, I must offer other explanations as well. You and Miss Sweeney might have made this whole thing up—forged the letter. There's nothing here to prove that it was sent to Ross Craigthorn. You don't have the envelope. You don't have the postmark you mentioned."

"Are you implying that we killed Ross?"

"I'm not implying anything. I'm just stating the possibilities. I have to. On the face of it, the letter seems genuine though, and it fits in with what Irma Black told me herself before she was killed."

Silently, he was cursing his own stupidity for not sticking closer to Irma Black, for not realizing at once that she was the key to the whole problem. Now it was too late. Now she was strangled by a telephone cord, and he had to start over. Had to, if necessary, go all the way to June, Nebraska, to dig into her past, and the past of Ross Craigthorn, and the past of the mysterious Victor, and try to fit it all together into some sort of absurd jigsaw puzzle.

And the hell of it was, he didn't know if he wanted to fit it together; because if MWA was involved, some good friend of his might be the man he sought. Someone he saw, and drank with, and talked to at every monthly meeting. He didn't want to face that. He didn't want to face the possibility of turning a friend over to the police. Maybe that's why Frank Jesset and Miss Sweeney seemed like logical suspects to him. Maybe it was just that he wanted it to be them.

"Is there anything else?" he asked.

"No," she answered. "We just wanted to show you the letter."

"I'd like to keep this, if I could."

They looked at each other again, and finally Miss Sweeney nodded. "All right. I've made a Xerox copy of it in the office. I do hope you'll use it with our best interests in mind. We don't want to get any more deeply involved in this than we have to."

"Don't worry," Barney said. "I'm only looking for a murderer. If you two are having an affair, you have nothing to fear from me." He had a sudden thought. "But tell me one thing. What about Craigthorn's wife?"

"She was in Mexico," Miss Sweeney answered. "Getting a divorce from him."

"Another woman?"

"Another man for her, according to the stories. An airline pilot."

He saw them to the door and waited while the elevator descended. When they'd gone, the letter was still there on the coffee table like some unanswered puzzle, needing to be read one more time. He thought about showing it to Susan Veldt, and then decided against it. He had to have some secrets from the girl. He certainly owed her nothing.

He phoned the airline ticket office and asked them how to get to June, Nebraska. It was not easy. But soon they had a route plotted by way of Chicago.

As soon as he could get clearance from the MWA board to pay for the trip, he'd be on his way.

119

Chapter Seventeen

SUSAN VELDT

She had very little trouble with Arthur Rowe over the expense account. He okayed the trip to June without a second thought. He was hot on this whole thing now, and she probably could have padded it enough to buy a mink coat without his ever noticing.

She packed just one suitcase, because she'd always traveled light, ever since her college days. One suitcase, with enough clothes for perhaps a two-day stay. Certainly nothing that June, Nebraska, had to offer would require more than that.

She was to meet Barney at MWA headquarters on Thursday morning, and she arrived early to find Betty Rafferty alone in the place, typing bills.

"It's dues time," Betty explained. "May first, every year. We get out the bills to the members, and then we sit back and wait around till the checks begin to drift in."

"Well, it breaks the routine, at least."

"Yes. It breaks the routine. It's sort of a bad time, though. You'd be amazed the number of really top writers who fall behind in their dues. Some of them are just procrastinators, like most writers. Others are just plain up against it. We had a fellow a few years back, a top name, and he was almost penniless. We carried him for as long as we could, and finally we had to drop him from the membership rolls. It's an odd thing in this business. I don't know if it's true of all writing, or just the mystery field, but you get people who have their names in magazines, publish a novel a year, win awards, and still fall behind in their dues. You can do all that, you know, and still make less than five thousand a year. And that's not enough to support a wife and family—not in New York, at least."

She went back to her typing, and Susan strolled over to look at the bookshelves. Mysteries, all mysteries. She regretted not having read more of them. Perhaps she should have read them in her youth. She had the impression that mysteries were for youth—college days, perhaps. Ross Craigthorn had said he'd started reading mysteries young, and she'd had a roommate in college who absolutely devoured them, starting with paperbacks, then going on to hardbounds, getting all the latest Agatha Christies and Rex Stouts and Ellery Queens as they appeared. The books would line her shelves, interspersed with works on political science and religious dogma. Though realizing they must have something to offer, Susan herself had never entered the world of mysteries, not till she'd read Barney's novel. They were an escape, she imagined, and she had nothing yet to escape from. Now, perhaps, she should be trying it.

Soon Barney arrived with his suitcase, looking happily refreshed. There was something about him, something she would have to face some day. But not quite yet.

"Well, we're off," he told Betty. "You know the motel we'll be at. You can reach us there at any time."

Betty looked up from her typewriter, suddenly sarcastic. "I won't call too late at night. I wouldn't want to disturb you two."

Susan snorted and led the way through the door. She certainly didn't want this to appear as any sort of an assignation, some lovers' trip halfway across the country, and she feared that's what some of them were thinking. Maybe it was all a scheme on Barney's part to compromise her, get her to spend the night with him. She remembered how it had been last Saturday night, when he'd tried something of the sort at her apartment.

Or had he? Was it only her own frigidity that made every male advance seem like some obscure plot against her? Maybe he just wanted to sleep with her. Maybe it was all as simple as that.

They caught a morning flight to Chicago, sitting next to each other, mostly in silence. She, reading the latest novel by John Updike; he, intent on a paperbound anthology of science-fiction stories edited by Hans Stefan Santesson.

"I didn't know you mystery writers read science fiction," she commented at one point.

"Have to see what's going on in the other fields. There are times when mystery and fantasy aren't that far apart. Some books manage to combine the best of both worlds. Ira Levin's bestselling novel, *Rosemary's Baby*, a couple of seasons ago was a prime example. It was, perhaps, a mystery, in the truest sense of the word. A mystery, as the term was used in the Middle Ages, for morality plays like *Everyman*."

"My! You're so educated!"

He grunted and went back to the book, then had a second thought and looked up at her again. "You should try some mysteries, or fantasy, occasionally. Updike is great, a great writer, but you should keep up with other fields of writing, too."

"Don't you think mystery writers are contributing toward some of the violence in the country today?"

He snorted and reached for a cigarette. "No. Not really. There's a theory, in fact, that we actually serve as an outlet for a good deal of the violence in this world. I won't go along with that, necessarily, but I do think we provide a something that is a part of modern life. There is and always will be violence. In children's books, in adult books, in every medium of entertainment. There is violence in Shakespeare, violence in the Bible. There was a murder in the Garden of Eden, remember?"

"I remember," she said.

"I don't think that we exploit it unduly. In fact, the true classic whodunit can have very little violence. Read an Agatha Christie—or most any of the top British writers,

122

and you'll see what I mean. The puzzle is the thing. The mysteries of the thirties had very little violence, except of course for practitioners like Hammett and Chandler. Though I'm not condemning them by any means, because they were masters in the field. But my point is that the mystery story can be many things, and violence is certainly not a necessity. There's nothing less violent than some of your good British mysteries. In fact there are a number of short stories by Agatha Christie which don't even concern murder."

"Well, I guess I didn't start reading them soon enough," she said. "Thanks to a course of instruction by Mr. Barney Hamet, maybe I'll learn it all without reading any of them."

"You said once you read mine."

"Did I say that? I can't remember the plot too well now."

"Come on. Let's have the truth! I'm a vain writer, or hadn't you noticed?"

"All right. I read one. The one about the undertaker killing all the people. Now don't tell me that wasn't violent."

"I wasn't commenting on my own work. That one was a bit bloody, I'll admit. I had a possibility of a screen sale to an independent producer. The deal fell through, but I guess I had that in mind when I was piling up the corpses. You know the sort of thing they like. Or used to like, at least. Before the latest clean-up campaign."

Each of them returned to their books. But only temporarily, for the spark of conversation had started. They went on from mysteries to politics, to the MWA organization, and the fight for better contracts for mystery writers. Barney outlined a bit about the beginnings of the group, in that final year of World War II. He mentioned people like Baynard Kendrick and Edward D. Radin and Anthony Boucher, who had done so much for the organization in those early years in New York and northern California and the other chapters.

"Are you going to visit the Chicago chapter while you're there?" Susan asked.

"There won't really be time between planes. I might call one or two people."

He did have time for just one call while they were on the ground, to an old friend he hadn't seen for years. Then they were airborne again, bound for Lincoln, a city he'd never visited. From there it was still more than an hour's drive to June, a town of a few thousand people in the southeast corner of the state.

Chapter Eighteen

BARNEY HAMET

His first view of June, Nebraska, came as their rented blue Ford topped a small hill and started down the other side. It was countryside. That was the best word to describe it. Fields, ripe with rich brown earth, being plowed by farmers driving massive yellow tractors. In other fields the spring planting was already completed. Perhaps wheat, or corn, oats or barley. Corn, he supposed. There was a sign by the side of the road with a large ear of corn on it, together with the name of some processor. Something to signify that this field would grow better ears and bigger kernels. As high, he supposed, as an elephant's eye. Nebraska, after all, wasn't that far from Oklahoma.

"Nice country," Susan Veldt remarked from the seat at his side.

"Great country. Great."

"A bit of sarcasm there, Mr. Hamet?"

"A city boy at heart."

"That's a cow over there—that big brown thing."

"Sure." He slowed the car to a stop and called to a muscular young man on a tractor. "Say, fella, can you direct us to the newspaper office in June?"

"No newspaper in June. Haven't had a newspaper in ten years." He eyed them with open curiosity.

"Well, I guess it's the old newspaper we want, then. Where might we find its editor, or somebody like that?"

"Gee . . . I guess you want Mrs. Phillips at the general store and post office."

Barney agreed. "I guess we want Mrs. Phillipps."

The young man's directions took them to the combination general store and post office, at a crossroads where the paving was beginning to crack and the dust from a dry spring was rising along the roadway in both directions.

Barney went in and talked to Mrs. Phillipps, a middle-aged woman as dry and wrinkled as the road outside.

"The editor of the newspaper, he said. "The newspaper that used to be published here ten or so years ago."

"Oh, that editor is gone! He fooled around too much with the ladies," she said, perhaps a bit sad that she hadn't been one of them. "I don't really know where you'd find any information about it."

"Back copies is what I was thinking of."

"Oh, no back copies! Who'd ever keep back copies of a little weekly paper that went out of business ten years ago?"

"Do you have a sheriff?"

"Well, there's a county sheriff, of course, but he's not in June. He's over at the county seat. There's nothing in June—nothing at all."

But there had been at one time, Barney thought. "We're looking for information about Irma Black."

"Well, why didn't you say so in the first place? Irma. I know Irma. She had a little farm just outside of town, until her husband died. She's all alone now. She went to New York a month or so back. Haven't heard anything from her since. She hasn't even written to her old friends."

"Irma Black is dead," he told her. "I'm sorry."

"Dead? Irma, dead? My God . . . I wonder if it was just being so heartbroken about living alone in the world. You know, us country people are funny that way. We live lonely lives, but then we get attached to somebody and when that somebody is gone, sometimes we just crumple up like an autumn leaf and blow away. I wonder if that's what happened to Irma."

"That's not what happened to Irma. She was strangled,

126

I'm afraid."

"Irma! In New York! I suppose so. Was she raped? Grabbed in an alley and raped and strangled?"

"No. In her apartment. And she wasn't raped."

"Terrible city! Terrible! Why she wanted to go there was beyond me! She said there were some friends that could give her money. What's money to her now that she's dead?"

"You don't know who the friends were? What their names were? Anything about them?"

"No, I don't know. She never mentioned any names. I wasn't that friendly with her. I just saw her when she came to get her mail."

"Did she ever receive mail from New York?"

"No. Never."

"From any place else? Any place far away?"

"No. Nothing but the usual junk. Her whole world was here."

"What about her past?" Barney asked. "Did you know her when she was young?"

"Not really. Before she was married, you mean? No, Irma wasn't the sort whose childhood you ever thought about."

"But she must have had one," Barney said. "She didn't grow up here in June?"

"In the area. Maybe over in the next town, or across the state line. I don't know."

"Was Black her maiden name?"

"Yes. Her husband's name was Tyron, I believe. I didn't know him very well."

Barney glanced around at Susan, who was busy choosing a candy bar after the long, hungry ride from Lincoln. He took out his wallet and slipped five dollars across the counter to the woman. "Come on, now. You can do better than that. You said you didn't know Irma Black at all before her marriage. Yet you knew the name right away. You knew it was her maiden name. How did you know that?"

"Well, she was using it again after her husband died." But the woman was flustered. Her hands were flying—trying to keep occupied. She looked at the five dollar bill, and then away. "I don't know anything, really!"

"Irma's dead, and whatever you tell me can't harm her

now."

"Really, I don't know anything," she said. "I never speak ill of living or dead. Go and talk to the sheriff."

"I guess I'll do just that," he told her. "Come on, Susan."

Outside, she pressed him for information. "What did you find out?"

"Nothing—except that there is something to find out. We just have to dig for it a little more deeply."

"Leave it to me," she said. "I'm being a sort of Watson, aren't I?"

"You mean you really read Sherlock Holmes once in your youth?"

"I saw a movie," she admitted. "It was pretty good. All about a big dog who killed people."

"See what you can find out," he said.

He left her and strolled down the main street, past a little white Methodist church that seemed to be boarded up. Whatever happened to all those Methodists, he wondered. He came at last to a blacksmith's shop, left over from another era. A new building had been constructed around back, for the sale of farm machinery. The horse had truly given way to the tractor here.

He strolled around till he found someone, a young man who seemed more the used-car-salesman type than the village blacksmith of old.

"Do you still shoe horses?" Barney asked.

"You got a horse to be shod, mister? We'll do it."

"You know a woman named Irma Black?"

"The one whose husband died?"

"That's right."

"No. I don't know her."

"You knew the name."

"I know the names of fifty people who live around here. Her husband used to deal with us before he died. She stopped farming. Probably sold the place, for all I know."

"Thanks," Barney said.

He went back to the car and drove down the road in search of Susan. She was in the phone booth at the general store.

"Calling back to New York," she said when she'd

128

finished. "After all, they pay me, you know."

"Yes. I know." But he wasn't happy about it.

"Mr. Rowe was wondering one thing."

"Oh? What was that?"

"How many people at MWA knew you were coming out here with me?"

"It was no big secret. I had to talk it over with the board of directors yesterday to get their approval for the trip. They all knew."

"That man that won the award—Max Winters. Has he gone back to California?"

"I don't really know, to tell you the truth. He was supposed to fly back on Monday, but I know he stayed over an extra day or two. I'm not sure just where Max is now. Why do you ask?"

"I thought I saw someone that looked like him at the Chicago airport while you were in the men's room. I meant to mention it to you."

"It could have been Max. He might have been changing planes."

"They have a direct flight to California, though, don't they?"

"Yes. But you never know. Maybe he was stopping off to see some old relative, or a girlfriend. Max used to be quite a swinger in his younger days."

"You've known him a long time?"

"What is this? A quiz or something? Sure, I've known Max a long time. Fifteen, twenty years. Isn't that a long time? Come on. I thought you were questioning people, not calling New York. A great Watson you'd make!"

"Where to now?" she asked, climbing into the car.

"Let's go see that sheriff at the county seat."

They drove in to the county seat, found the sheriff's office, and sat in a plain little ice-beige room, waiting until the sheriff himself put in an appearance. His clothes sagged badly on him, as if he'd recently been ill and lost a great deal of weight. He walked the same way. He was a wasted man, on his last legs. Perhaps that was the sort Barney wanted. Perhaps he'd have memories of those older days.

"Sheriff, I'm Barney Hamet from New York, and this is Miss Veldt. We're here investigating some murders that took place there. One of the victims, a woman named Irma Black, lived over in June. We were told that you might be able to tell us something about her. Especially about her early life."

"Irma Black? I know the name. What was it you wanted to know?"

Barney looked at the sheriff's wrinkled hands. "I'm not exactly sure. We talked to the postmistress over there. She threw out a few hints. It would be something in Irma's background. Something that happened twenty or twenty-five years ago. I think perhaps a crime of some sort. A crime involving two men."

The sheriff squinted at them. "You come all the way from New York to ask me about that? That's old stuff now. Didn't happen here, anyway. Happened across the state line. Different state entirely. Here." He pulled down a map on the wall, and pointed his shaky finger at the area where Nebraska, Kansas, Iowa and Missouri all came together. "See? Irma lived near June. Lived near June all her life. But she worked over here—in Claxton. At the Claxton Trust Company."

"A bank?" Barney asked.

"Sure, a bank. What else? She was a teller there. Back just after the war. She was a young girl then. In her mid-twenties, I suppose."

"What happened at the bank?"

"What usually happens at banks? It got robbed. A gunman came in one day and robbed the bank, and kidnapped Irma as a hostage."

"Oh," Barney leaned forward, intently now, sure that he had come to the end of his search. "One bandit?"

"One in the bank. Another in the car."

"How long did they hold Irma a prisoner?"

"That was the funny part of it. They kept her a week. A whole week. And then finally they brought her back and dropped her."

"Had she been harmed?"

"I couldn't tell you that. I wasn't that close to the case. You could probably find a report of it somewhere, though, if you really wanted it."

"The two men. What happened to them?"

"What do you mean, what happened to them?"

"Were they ever caught?" Barney asked, holding his breath while he waited for the answer.

"Sure they were caught. About a month later. They tried to crash a police roadblock and they were both killed instantly."

"Oh."

"We know how to handle law and order out in this part of the country, Mr. Hamet. Don't you worry about that. You New York fellas can learn a lot from us."

"Yeah," Barney said. "I'm sure we could. I'm sure we all could. Come on, Susan."

They finally found a library and he put Susan to work scouring the newspapers for the month in question. It had been the summer of '47 when it happened—in July. And before they'd been there too long Susan called to him from behind a pile of bound newspapers. "Here it is, Barney. I've got the whole story here. Complete with a picture of Irma Black."

He leaned over her shoulder and read it. The thing had been big news, all right. BANK BANDIT KIDNAPS TELLER; EIGHT-STATE ALARM OUT FOR GUNMAN AND ACCOMPLICE. And he read further:

A lone masked gunman, brandishing a sawed-off shotgun, entered the main office of the Claxton Trust Company just before closing time Tuesday and escaped with nearly thirty thousand dollars, taking a girl teller with him as hostage.

Victim of the kidnapping was Irma Black, twenty-six, a resident of June, Nebraska, who had worked at the bank for two years. Police immediately ordered roadblocks up on all major highways, and issued an eight-state alarm for the fugitives and their hostage. Although only one man entered the bank, witnesses said another was waiting in a car, which sped off immediately.

There was more, much more, including a picture of Irma's house and an interview with her worried parents. The story continued for a full week with veiled hints that the girl teller would not be found alive. But on the eighth day, the headlines had a cheerful note: IRMA BLACK SAFE! RELEASED NEAR HOME BY TWO BANK BANDITS!

There followed the usual interviews, in which she said she had been well treated, but had been kept blindfolded most of the time and could give no description of her abductors. She said only that they had talked in southern accents and spoke once of going to Mexico.

"What do you make of it?" Susan asked. "Could this be the thing? Could this be what she was blackmailing Ross Craigthorn for?"

But Barney only grunted and kept looking through the papers until he found the later news item the sheriff had mentioned. Acting on a tip, police had thrown up a roadblock near a farm on the other side of Lincoln. A car with two men in it had tried to crash the roadblock, and the police had riddled it with bullets. The men were later identified as Tom Clancy and his brother, Rick, two small-time criminals who had both served prison terms for assault and armed robbery.

Irma Black was brought to view the bodies in the morgue, and although she had previously stated she was blindfolded during her captivity, she now said she believed the Clancy brothers to have been her abductors. Two days later the police announced that money found at the farm where the brothers were hiding was "almost certainly" part of the loot from the Claxton bank robbery. The case was marked closed.

"Well," Susan observed, "they were running from something. That's for sure."

Barney grunted and turned back a few pages. "So, there were a couple of other robberies that month. Here's a general store that was robbed, and a gas station. It could have been almost anything. It didn't have to be the Claxton bank. I'd hardly call this enough evidence to convict. It just got the local police off the hook."

"But if Irma Black suspected Ross Craigthorn, then she must have known all along it wasn't the Clancy brothers. If she knew that, why did she lie to the police? What was in it for her?"

"Maybe just a week of fun that she wanted to remember. Maybe it was the most exciting week of her life. Maybe it was the only week she ever had a man who loved her."

"Oh, come on, Barney! Now you're really reaching for it!"

"Am I? She opened her apartment door to someone. She let that person get near enough to strangle her with a telephone cord. What does that tell us? It tells us that it was someone she knew, someone she'd known very well. And someone she could trust, or thought she could trust. Even after Ross Craigthorn's murder."

"You believe that, don't you?"

"Let's go back and read these interviews with her. Dig out anything we can."

They read for another twenty minutes, side by side in the library. It wasn't until the very last paragraph of one of the interviews that their search was rewarded.

"She said they called each other by nicknames," Susan pointed. "It's right here in the story, but it doesn't say what the nicknames were."

"Well, we'll get that quickly enough. I have a feeling about it. I think I know what they were."

They talked, next, to the district attorney's office. The transcripts of the investigation were buried in files twenty-two years old, and they waited on a hard wooden bench for the better part of an afternoon until a bespectacled little man came out, blowing dust from a file folder. "The Irma Black kidnapping. Is that what you wanted? And the bank robbery?"

"That's right," Barney said.

"Well, of course, I can only show you the things that are a matter of public record, you understand. You have no official capacity."

"I just want you to answer one question for me. One of the news stories mentions nicknames. I want to know what those nicknames were."

"Nicknames? Nicknames of the Clancy brothers?"

"Nicknames of the two men who kidnapped Irma Black."

"Let's see here. Nicknames . . . here it is, in her statement:

They kept me blindfolded all of the time, and tied me to a chair. I never really saw them at all, except in the beginning, when they first got me into the car. They didn't talk much to each other, and when they did, they used nicknames. One was Caesar and the other was Raven. They were funny names. That help you mister?"

"That helps me," Barney said. "Caesar and Raven. Does she say which was which?"

"No, I don't . . . yeah . . . wait a second. Here. Here's something. *Caesar was the one waiting in the car at the robbery scene.* I guess that means Raven was the guy who held up the bank."

"Yeah. It figures," Barney said. "Thanks a lot, mister."

They went back to the motel near June, where they were spending the night, and Barney slumped down on the bed. He stretched out full length, blowing cigarette smoke at the ceiling.

"Well, that gives it to us, doesn't it?"

"Gives what to us?" she asked him.

"Motive. It's a funny case. Usually in books, the motive is one of the last things to be discovered, but we've got it right here."

"You're implying that Ross Craigthorn was this Caesar?"

"Of course. It stands to reason, doesn't it? A couple of fellows, maybe just out of college, or out of the army, looking for thrills. And one of them decides to rob a bank. The other one stays in the car. Maybe he knows what's going on, or maybe he doesn't. But anyway, he's in it. He's in it pretty deep. And when they bring along a girl as hostage, he knows that it's big trouble for them both. So then, a couple of guys that didn't have anything to do with the robbery are killed, and the thing is blamed on them. Caesar and Raven go off to start new lives somewhere. It was just one fling. Something, I suppose, like Loeb and Leopold.

"Only it didn't go that far. They didn't kill the girl, though heaven knows what they did do to her. Anyway, she wasn't talking. And she kept their secret—however much she knew. She knew enough, though, to recognize Ross Craigthorn on television as one of them. He must have been the one driving the car. I don't think that even Craigthorn could have hoped to cop a plea to his great American public if he walked into a bank with a sawed-off shotgun. But with the statute of limitations long ago run out, he probably could have made it sound like a youthful prank. Especially if he was waiting outside all that time.

"But don't you see what this does? It gives our other man, the mysterious Mr. Raven, a nice motive. With Craigthorn telling the story, revealing that the Clancy brothers were innocent, he'd have to reveal that Raven was still around too. Even if he didn't tell anything else, even if he passed over Raven's present identity, don't you think the reporters would be digging? Raven, of course, would be in a more delicate position. He couldn't plead that he was sitting in a car. He was the one who was actually in there with that shotgun, scooping up the money, and kidnapping the girl. It would go a lot tougher on him, either at Irma Black's hands, or with the police and public. He was a dyed-in-the-wool criminal. A lot more culpable than Craigthorn, even though they were both involved. And he could probably still have been arrested on the kidnapping charge."

"I can see that, Barney, but does it do anything toward telling us who he is?"

"No, but we're only starting, girl! The next move is to find out all we can about Craigthorn's boyhood. Someone's going to know who he hung out with. Someone's going to know who his chums were. Maybe an army record, if they were in the army together. We can check and see who his college roommates were. I think we're on the trail now!"

"Raven and Caesar—what odd names! They don't really have anything in common, do they?"

Barney grunted. "What did you want them to have in common?"

"Well, Caesar is like Roman Empire. Did they have ravens back in Rome? Was that a raven on those staffs that the Roman legions used to carry?"

"I think it was probably an eagle. I don't know of any ravens before Poe." He hesitated. "Poe. Where did Poe get the idea for that raven?"

"What?"

"A thought just struck me. What time would it be back in New York now?"

She glanced at her watch. "Around four o'clock."

"Get on the phone and call New York, see if we can reach Harry Fox at his office. If anybody knows where Poe got the idea for the raven, it's Harry Fox."

"You think he got it from Julius Caesar?"

"I don't know, but I want to find out."

They sent out for sandwiches, and sat around for a while. Harry was out of his office, but his answering service promised he would return the call as soon as he could. They waited another hour before it finally came in.

"Yeah, this is Harry. That you, Barney? What in the hell are you doing out there, spending all of MWA's money? You and that girl—I'll bet you're camped out in a motel somewhere."

"That's just about right, Harry. We're in a place called June, Nebraska. Ever hear of it?"

"June, Nebraska. There's no such place!"

"Look on a map sometime, Harry. Listen, I need to know something, and you're the one who can tell me. So get the computer memory going. Edgar Allan Poe. *The Raven*. Okay?"

"Gotchya."

"Where did Poe get the idea for *The Raven*? Was there any raven in past literature? Anything at all?"

"I'll bet you think you're stumping me, don't you?" Harry said. "You should know Poe is my field."

"That's why we called you halfway across the country. Give out with the information."

"Well, Poe got the idea from Dickens. From the raven in Dickens' novel, *Barnaby Rudge*."

"Can you document that?"

"Sure. Poe reviewed *Barnaby Rudge* and said that more should have been done with the raven. Then a few years later, in the *New York Evening Mirror* for January 29,

136

1845, Poe published his own poem, *The Raven*. How's that, huh?"

"*Nevermore*," Barney said. "What else have you got?"

"Well, the *Barnaby Rudge* thing is the only certainty. But there are a couple of other ravens that Poe was familiar with. Walpole's *Reminiscences*, chapter two, has a passage referred to by Byron to the effect that the Duchess of Kendal believed that the soul of George the First returned to her in the form of a large raven."

"Now, come on," Barney said. "Where you getting this stuff from?"

"Okay, here's another for you, if you're still doubting me. There's a raven mentioned in Wilson's *Noctes Ambrosianae*."

"Okay. Forget it. Forget it. I'll settle for Barnaby Rudge's raven. Thanks a lot, Harry."

"When will you two be back from your little love-in?"

Barney snorted. "A day or two, depending on how it goes. And I don't mean what you think. How's the weather in New York?"

"Not bad. A bit of rain this morning, but it's sunny now."

Barney hung up and conveyed Harry Fox's information to Susan. "Well," she said, "what does that give you? A raven from Charles Dickens. That's no better than the raven from Poe, is it?"

"I don't know. Do you have a list of the people that were at the dinner?"

"It just so happens," she began, digging into the attaché case she'd brought along. It was a flowery sort of thing that no man would have been caught dead with, but somehow it summed up Susan Veldt's personality. Flowers on an attaché case. He hadn't seen her with it before the trip, and he supposed that she usually left it in the office, settling for the notebook in her purse. "Here's the mimeographed list that they passed out at the dinner."

He started running down the names. "Take a couple of pages. Look for the names of anybody at the dinner who might have any connection with a Dickens character."

"Isn't that going a little too far? You mean that Craigthorn, in his dying breath, smashed that Raven so that

137

you'd get the connection between the raven and Poe, and Dickens and BARNABY RUDGE and another raven, and some other characters in Dickens? I can't imagine even a dying man going to such lengths."

"I'll agree it's farfetched, but we've got to start somewhere. Ross Craigthorn smashed that Raven because it was the only thing handy. He wasn't telling us exactly who killed him. He was just giving us a steer in the right direction. If Craigthorn was Caesar, and his killer was Raven . . ."

His voice trailed off as he scanned the list. There were lots of names. He recognized a lady lawyer who could have reminded him of Shakespeare's Portia—but that wasn't exactly Dickens. There were no Scrooges on the list. Not even a Tiny Tim. A publisher named Muggins—was there a Muggins in Dickens somewhere? Muggins . . . he couldn't be sure. There were lots of Davids, but no Copperfield. A few Olivers, but no Twist. And certainly no Rudges, nor even any Barnabys. It was another blank wall.

"Okay," she said. "What now?"

"Now we try and find out where Ross Craigthorn grew up and went to school and stuff. We'll start checking all the schools in this area. You take some, and I'll take the rest." He remembered Irma Black's letter. "You might check the name Craig, too."

The project occupied most of the next day, and it was Susan who finally came up with a possibility. She phoned Barney at the district high school where he was checking, talking excitedly. "Barney, I think I've got something! There was a boy here called Ross Craig."

"What year did he graduate?"

"Just before the war. He went in the army then, and people lost sight of him. He could be the one we want."

"Okay," Barney said. "Look, put in a call to Amalgamated Broadcasting, and see what they've got on Craigthorn's biography. Or better still, call *The New York Times*, and have them read you the obit they ran on him last week. It seems to me they spoke of him as coming from the Midwest, but it was nowhere near June, Nebraska."

138

Toward evening they met to assemble their bits and pieces of information. The calls to New York had proved little. The *Times* obituary had come from Amalgamated Broadcasting information and press releases over the years. There was an article in *TV Guide* to be consulted, too, but they all were vague about Craigthorn's early years. A farm in Kansas seemed to be the best lead, but no specific town was mentioned. Nor was any high school.

He'd gotten out of the army in nineteen forty-five, and here was where the trail grew warmer. He'd attended college under the name of Ross Craigthorn at the University of Texas. There were more phone calls, and Barney debated for a time flying down to Texas.

"That's where the answer lies. I'm sure of it. Look, he was in college in late '45 and '46 and into '47. He met his partner there. They headed north in the summer of '47. Maybe with a car. Probably Craigthorn's car, since he was driving at the bank. They headed north, and the other boy got the idea of robbing the bank. Of taking Irma Black with them. Exactly what happened that week, we'll probably never know. But anyway, they were in the clear on it. The Clancy brothers got blamed, and Caesar and Raven headed for New York."

"Barney, do you really think Craigthorn would have admitted all this? To the nation? Admitted it, as apparently he was going to, at the Mystery Writers dinner?"

"Under the threat of blackmail? Yes. Irma Black wanted a hundred thousand dollars, and she obviously wouldn't stand still for much less. How much was taken in the bank robbery? Around thirty thousand, wasn't it? Craigthorn could have made a contrite speech, explained that he wasn't directly involved in the bank robbery, and even sent back the thirty thousand dollars. They couldn't indict him for anything at this late date, unless it was as an accessory to the kidnapping, and that would be hard to prove. His conscience would be clear, and he would have gotten out of it for less than a third of what Irma Black wanted. It's exactly the sort of thing Craigthorn would have done. It would even have given him a good story, and loads of free publicity. Boyish escapade! A prank!"

"Maybe," she said, not entirely convinced.

"We've still got to track him down. Someone here must know him. Ross Craig. Let's see if there are any Craigs in the phone book."

There was only one Craig in the county telephone directory—Schuyler Craig. Though it was nearly dark, they drove over to his house to see him.

He was a man of eighty or more years, and though he held himself well, the shadow of death was already creeping over his features. He sat on the darkened front porch and talked of the old days. Very little of the present. Nothing of the future. But luckily for them, he had a perfect memory. And luckily for them, he had been Ross Craig's uncle.

"Sure," he said. "Sure, I know he went to New York. Terrible thing about him getting killed."

"You knew he was killed? You knew he was Ross Craigthorn?"

"Well, I see him on the television, don't I? Of course I recognized him! Craigthorn was the family name way back. That's probably why he reverted to it. Some of us just shortened it to Craig, that's all."

"You knew him. What can you tell us about him?"

The old man studied his gnarled knuckles. "Well, I can tell you anything you want to know! He was a good boy. You know, the usual things—skipping school, going off with the crowd, but a good boy deep down. He went in the army and was a regular hero during the war. It's funny! Of all the things I've seen about him, he never talked much about his boyhood. Kept it like a big secret. One article even said he was brought up in Kansas, and I sure as hell knew that wasn't true! I used to bounce him on my knee when he was a baby! Now, he got big—made all that money. But it didn't do him much good, did it? He died anyway. Just like all of us."

He stared out beyond the trees, possibly at the sunset, possibly at something neither of the others would see. "Just like all of us."

"Mr. Craig," Susan urged, trying to lead the conversation, "we're interested especially in his college days. He went to the University of Texas, didn't he?"

"That's right. The University of Texas. Star student there."

"Did he ever come up to see you any of the times while he was in college?"

"Sure, during the summer he came. Every summer! He'd drive up here, sometimes with a friend."

"Yes, a friend! That's what we need to know. Mr. Craig, was it always the same friend?"

"No. Different boys. Different boys."

"Do you remember their names?"

"Oh, I've got a good memory. But I don't know if it's that good or not."

"Mr. Craig, he started college in the fall of 1945. In the summer of '47, he would have finished his sophomore year. With allowances for his army service, he would have been in his mid-twenties. The summer of '47, he came up here with another boy. We need to know the name of that other boy."

"You're asking an awful lot! An awful lot." The old man continued staring, and for a moment Barney thought he might be blind. But then he looked back at them and his eyes livened a bit. "Of course there's the album. In those days I used to mark the names on the pictures, and I took pictures a lot. My wife was still alive then, and she liked them. We liked to look at them. Come into the house for a minute. Maybe we'll be lucky. Maybe we'll find something."

Susan held a stack of magazines dating back to the nineteen-forties, and tried to brush the dust from them with a cloth, while old Craig dug deep into the bottom of a sadly worn cedar chest.

"Yeah. The photo albums. Here they are. Ah, here's a picture of Ross. See him? Recognize him? He didn't change that much."

He had changed quite a bit, but they could recognize him. Ross Craig was Ross Craigthorn, and there was no doubt about it now. A picture of him in an army uniform, smiling shyly at the camera, with that same expression they'd grown to know from the late news every night. Barney had rarely watched the new show, but still he recognized the tight lips and piercing eyes. Another photo showed him with a girl. His wife, perhaps. The one that was divorcing him at the time of his murder.

"Was he engaged in '47?" Barney asked.

"No. He didn't meet the girl till later. After college. Here! Here's a picture of one fellow! This was an army buddy. Summer of '45. See, I've got the date right on the back. July 20, 1945. It was just after they were out. Those were the days. I remember, they were still here when we dropped the atom bomb on the Japs, and it all came to an end, sudden like. All those years of fighting, and then it just ended."

"I don't know if this would be the boy we want. Something later."

"1946?"

"No. Later than that."

"Summer '47. July of '47. Yeah. Here's one. Took it out under the old willow tree. Damn limbs are hanging down so long you can hardly see them. He had one boy with him that summer. Sure. Drove up with him from the University. Here they are. Clear as anything. That's my wife there in the middle. And that's Ross, on the right."

Barney was staring hard at the boy on the left, but it was useless. The willow hung too low. And perhaps his face had moved just at the critical moment. There was only a blur of white. Unidentifiable. "What was his name?" Barney asked.

The old man turned over the photo and pointed a knobby finger at the handwritten caption. "Name was Jones. Victor Jones."

Chapter Nineteen

Victor Jones

He'd never thought he'd come back. Not back to June, Nebraska.

The place held too many memories for him, pleasant and unpleasant. It wasn't a matter of never going home again, because June, Nebraska had never really been his home. But he'd spent a lot of time here, especially in the summers when he and Ross Craigthorn would drive up from the university. Yes. Those were the days. Summer days. Driving north through Oklahoma, over flat country, farmland, past the corn fields, picking up occasional hitchhikers to joke with, stopping in run-down hotels, looking for girls. They'd been buddies then. Jones and Craig. That was a damn good life.

He remembered the first time Ross had ever mentioned June, Nebraska. He hadn't believed that such a place existed, even after he'd seen it on the map. They'd driven up there on Thanksgiving vacation in the fall of '46. That had been the first time. They'd gotten to know a few of the people in the town—Ross renewing old friendships, and Victor making new ones. They were just two guys then, out for the hell of it. They both read mysteries a lot. Perhaps that was what had attracted them to each other at the university. They discussed all the latest plot twists on the road north.

It was on one of their drives that Victor Jones had proposed the great bank robbery. He remembered it now as if it were yesterday. "You know, Ross, there's a lot of money to be made in these little towns. We roll through them, and we see the banks, and we keep going. You walk in there with a shotgun. It wouldn't even have to be loaded. You just walk in there with a shotgun, and you tap it on the counter, and they hand you all that money."

"You're going to be a big outlaw, huh?"

"Maybe. Maybe it's better than going to college for all your life, and getting out, and making a hundred dollars a week."

"Times will get better," Ross always said. "They'll get better without us having to turn to crime."

"Maybe it's not so much the money. Maybe I just want to do something for the hell of it. Just to see if I could pull it off. The two of us could pull it off, Ross. I know we could."

"I'm not getting involved in any of your screwy schemes! You read too many of those books."

"It's not the books. It's not the books that give me the ideas. I got the ideas already. Maybe that's why I read the books."

"Well, try something else. then. You know, in the books the killer always gets caught in the last chapter."

But Victor Jones had only sighed. "I don't think I would, Ross! I don't think I'd get caught in the last chapter. I think I could be the greatest criminal in the world if I put my mind to it. Just like I could be the greatest writer. Or newspaperman."

But the talks had never gotten anywhere. There was a return trip to June at Christmas. And then plans for the big summer ahead. They would travel north—perhaps work on a farm Ross knew, stay there for a time, and then swing back south again for the fall term at Texas. It sounded good.

That summer, the summer of '47 when it all happened, was the last time that Victor Jones had visited June, Nebraska. After that day, and the week that followed, something happened to their friendship. He thought at times that Ross might actually have been frightened of him. Frightened of his potency. Of his drive. And so, they drifted apart.

Now, as Victor Jones parked the rented car down the darkened street in June, he knew he had come home again. Home, to the home that was not his home. Home, to the only living relative Ross Craigthorn still had. Uncle Schuyler.

He'd thought the old man must be dead. He'd thought anyone must be dead after all this time. And he'd been startled to learn from Irma that he was alive. Alive and well, or as well as a man could be in his mid-eighties.

He patted the beard on his chin as he stared through the windshield at the house down the block, and saw the car in the driveway. Could they have gotten here before him? Was that possible? Could they have beaten him again, as they did to Irma Black's apartment?

Irma had reminded him of the old uncle's habit of taking pictures, and that was what had spurred him on. Pictures can be deceptive. They can show only a blur or a blob—or they can show the whole of a person's life. They had left June before he ever saw the prints, and he did not know what the pictures would reveal. He did not know if, looking at them, the secret of his whole life might be revealed to all the world.

And so he had come back to June to find out. He stood in the darkness on the quiet street, against the rough bark of a maple tree, watching the house, and waiting. He waited a long time before he saw them come out, but he recognized them at once, even at a distance—Barney Hamet and Susan Veldt. He considered the necessity for killing them both—tried rationally to study the problem. But he knew in a portion of his mind that he was beyond rationality now. The crime of his youth had led to one murder. And that had led to a second murder. Now must it lead to two more murders? Would there be no end to it? What had become of him in these past weeks?

But perhaps it was destined to be like this. Perhaps his whole life had been leading to this point. The murder of Ross Craigthorn had been carefully planned, intricately

145

evolved, using an electronic device. A foolproof murder, really, and one on which he prided himself. It would have made a fitting plot device for a mystery novel.

But with Irma Black, he'd started to come apart. Of course he'd gone there to kill her—at least in that dark portion of his mind. But he had gone unarmed and unplanned—unprogrammed, perhaps. He had gone there and seized the only instrument that came to hand, a telephone. Hitting her, striking her with it, finally strangling her with its cord. Yes, perhaps this was the way murderers evolved. A carefully planned crime gave way to a spur-of-the-moment offense.

And now . . . now what? He had not come to June unprepared. He carried a gun in his belt, a Colt .45 that had been in his possession since those distant days of World War II. He tried to remember now where he'd gotten the gun. He'd never himself seen combat. Perhaps it had been the final prize in some all-night poker game, or the last pawn of a desperate young G.I. He'd fired it on only one occasion, back in the late forties, when he and Ross were up at the old farm.

But it was the gun that had been with him that day in the bank—the gun in his belt to back up the sawed-off shotgun that he'd plunked against the teller's cage when he asked for the money. The .45 had been there too, because Ross didn't want it—didn't want to carry it, or touch it. He'd never had to fire the .45, or even draw it. It had been resting there against his stomach, in his belt. And the cold pressure of it spurred on his crime. He'd showed it to Irma once, during that week. Showed it to her, not threatened her with it—because she did not need threats. Irma Black had been more than cooperative. What had started as a kidnapping had become a week of vague pleasure, of day-long couplings on the bed in the old farm house, broken only by the occasional need to eat or sleep.

Irma Black had liked it. She'd liked him, and later, while he rested, she had even liked Ross, for a time. Funny thing how lives worked out. He would have been willing to bet that she'd have ended up a neurotic prostitute, torn by guilt feelings. But nothing of the sort had happened. She'd married a reasonably dignified and prosperous farmer, and apparently lived a possibly contented life, until his recent death. Only then had she thought back to the past. Back to that week of sin and some sort of salvation. Only then had she decided on blackmail. Of renewing old acquaintances.

She had, to the best of his knowledge, never told anyone of the more bizarre pleasures of her kidnapping. She had, in fact, told the police upon her release that she had not been harmed—that she'd been kept blindfolded and tied, but untouched—for the entire week. They believed her, of course. There was no reason to examine her or to doubt her word. And she'd done them the further service of falsely identifying the brothers killed at the police roadblock.

Victor Jones often thought about the Clancy brothers— wondered what crime they had been fleeing from in their own minds when they crashed through into a barrage of gunfire. He owed them a debt of thanks, in a way. And back then, he'd thought of visiting their grave, or sending flowers, or making some gesture of that sort. Only prudence had dissuaded him.

Now it was twenty-two years later, and the .45 automatic was pressing against his stomach again, where he had liked to carry it in the old days. Ross, the sort whose mother had told him not to wear sneakers when he was young, had been horrified by this, had even mentioned the remote possibility of the gun's going off, and doing grievous damage to Victor's private parts. But that sort of thing only happened in scare stories conjured up by overly protective females. Never in real life.

Victor Jones returned to his car and drove slowly behind the two he sought. There was no need now for visiting the uncle. It was too late for that. Barney Hamet would have the picture, if there was a picture. Barney Hamet and Susan Veldt would know the truth, if there was a truth.

He feared for a time they might check out of the motel at once, without spending the night. But already it was after ten o'clock, and he saw from the way they parked the car, talked for a time, and then went in to the motel, that they were settling in for the night.

He waited a while longer, until it was almost eleven, and then strolled by the car casually, stroking his beard as if deep in thought. Her flowery attaché case was in the back seat of the locked automobile, along with some folders of Barney's. It was just possible that the pictures, or any other information they'd obtained, were in there.

He would look there first. Then, if necessary, he would use the gun. One more time. Just one more time. Just these two, and then his secret would be safe. He needn't kill again, ever. Just these two. Just two bullets, and don't think about it afterwards.

Do it, and don't think about it.

Chapter Twenty

BARNEY HAMET

They were in his room, and Barney was flopped on the bed, staring at the ceiling.

"All right," he said to Susan, "what do we have? A bank robbery, the kidnapping of a teller named Irma Black, a blurred photograph of someone named Victor Jones. Did you check with the University?"

She nodded from her chair. "I talked to the dean of men, probably got him out of bed. He'll have his secretary go through old yearbooks first thing in the morning. I told him it was very important that we find a photograph of Victor Jones, and any information we could get about him. He's going to call us back here, tomorrow."

Barney glanced at his watch. It was nearly eleven. "Good. I'd like to catch an early afternoon plane back, if we could."

"Who do you think Victor Jones is, Barney? One of those people who were at the broadcast with you?"

"It almost has to be. I just hope it isn't . . ." He let the sentence drift off unfinished. Then after a moment, he asked, "Shouldn't you be going to your room? We don't want to cause talk."

"Are you kicking me out?"

"Why not? You kicked me out last Saturday."

"That was different."

"I don't know. Maybe, maybe not. I never know what to expect from you."

"Expect the worst, Barney," she said. She rummaged around in her purse for a pack of cigarettes.

Feeling gentlemanly, he went over and lit one for her.

"Where is this getting us, anyway?" he asked.

"Where is what getting us?"

"Where is any of this getting us? You know, Betty back at the office thinks we're sleeping together."

"Let her think it. Let her think anything she wants."

"Do you fear men that much? Or hate them?"

"I never met a man I didn't hate. Somebody said that once."

"I think you're misquoting it a bit. And I don't believe you anyway. You're not a bad-looking girl, Susan. Behind that phony sophistication there beats a heart of lead, or something."

"Let's not talk about me," she said.

"Let's. It's an interesting subject."

But the phone rang then, and she scooped it up. "Susan Veldt here." Very professional.

"Yes, professor . . . yes. I certainly appreciate your working so late on it. Oh . . . I see. Nothing at all? How about fraternity pictures? Underclassmen? Sports events? No, he didn't . . . I see. No, we've got one that's probably as good as what you have. But thanks very much, sir. Goodbye."

"That didn't sound very promising," Barney remarked.

"It wasn't. He stayed up and looked through his own set of yearbooks, but didn't find a thing. Victor Jones never graduated. Two years is all he put in. After that he just sort of dropped from sight. Went east, somebody said. Ross Craigthorn graduated, of course, under the name of Craig, but he was alone in his final two years. No Victor Jones. So where does that leave us?"

"No pictures at all?"

"No. The dean looked through all the underclassmen books. He was apparently absent for the photograph one year. They were just group things, of course, for undergraduates, and quite often didn't show everybody. If you'll remember your own college days, they weren't too fussy about who they got in, except for the seniors. He also checked fraternity pictures and sports events, but found nothing. There's just one picture of him in a group of sophomores, but I gather it's about as good as the one we've got. Nothing worth identifying. Not twenty-two years later, at least."

"Where's the picture we got from the uncle? Out in the car?"

"I think so. We left it there in my attaché case."

"I want to look at it again," he said.

He went downstairs quickly, out the side door of the motel and across to where the cars were parked. He was almost to their rented sedan when he saw the smashed side window. His muscles tensed. He glanced around, seeing no one, then went the rest of the way to the car. It was parked next to an identical blue Ford, probably rented from the same place, but the other car hadn't been touched.

The attaché case had been gone through quickly, as had his folders. The picture, for what little it was worth, was gone. Barney straightened things up, closed the back door, opened the front and brushed some of the glass from the seat.

Damn, he thought! So someone had followed them out here to June! And that someone could only be the mysterious Victor Jones.

It was a noise, a noise like a cinder scraping a shoe, that caused him to turn. He had only the briefest of glimpses. A figure—perhaps thirty feet away. A bearded man, outlined against the lights of the motel parking lot. A bearded man with a gun. Then Barney threw himself sideways as the gun roared, surprisingly loud. A .45, or something big. He felt the slug tear into the car next to him, actually shaking it with the impact.

"I'm armed!" Barney yelled, bluffing to the end. "Throw down your gun and give up!"

The .45 coughed again—louder this time, closer. The bullet chipped into the cinders by his feet. He couldn't see the man now. He was in the shadows, edging around to Barney's right, behind the car somewhere. In another moment he'd have Barney between his gun and the lights, and then it would be all over.

Barney dropped flat against the cinders and edged himself beneath the car next to his own. His only hope was to hold out for another moment of two. Even in a town like June, shots from a .45 were going to attract some attention pretty quickly. The guy couldn't stalk him out here for long. Already he heard someone shouting from the motel. "What's going on out there? What's going on?"

There was a scraping of cinders somewhere off to Barney's right—about two or three cars away. Maybe the bearded man was turning to run. Barney hopped up on hands and feet, ready to give chase, then thought better of it. There was no arguing with a .45. Not unarmed as he was.

He waited another moment, till the running footsteps receded, then went back to the motel.

Susan Veldt was there, her face full of apprehension. "What was it, Barney? What was it?"

"Someone took a shot at me. A man with a beard."

"Did you get a good look at him?"

"Only that." He leaned against the door frame. "He's gone now. But he broke into our car and got the picture."

"You mean the picture that the uncle gave you?"

"That's the one."

"Why could he have been after that? It doesn't show anything." She answered her own question. "But I don't suppose he knew that until he saw it."

"We'd better call the police. Report the whole thing and have them put a guard on the uncle's home for a day or two. We don't want him to end up the same way as Irma Black."

He called the police, then waited until a state highway patrol car came by, and answered a few routine questions from a bored trooper. There was a cursory inspection of the car and reports to be filled out about that. There were a few cigarette butts found along with the two ejected cartirdges, but they proved nothing except that the man might have stood there awhile, waiting.

The police left, and finally they were alone again.

"You've no idea who it was?"

"Yeah. I've got a damn good idea that it was the mysterious Victor Jones. But at this point that doesn't tell us too much we didn't already know."

"You said a beard."

"I'm not counting on its being real. There was something, though. Something familiar about him. Just the way he stood there. It reminded me of something, and I can't remember what."

"You really think he followed us out from New York?"

"That's the only explanation there is. And I think it's time we got back to New York. Any more research on the past of Victor Jones will have to be conducted from there. Give me the city any time. Towns like June are just too dangerous."

They flew back by way of Chicago on Saturday afternoon. The flight was smooth and uneventful, but by the time they had circled Kennedy Airport for an hour and finally landed, Barney was tired and depressed. He took Susan home to her apartment, and declined an invitation to come up, perhaps fearing a repetition of the previous Saturday evening.

Sunday was a lost day. It was the first weekend in May, warm and promising, and everyone he tried to call seemed off and away somewhere—wherever New Yorkers go on weekends when the weather is good. Finally he opened a beer and settled down to watch a Mets game on television, trying not to look at the half-completed short story in the typewriter. It had been there for more than a month now.

Monday was different.

He awoke early, and stood for a moment at the window of his apartment, staring out at the brownish haze that hung unmoving across the Manhattan skyline. Some sort of temperature inversion, caused by unusually warm weather for May. The meteorologists could all explain it, and the newspapers would print their explanations. It made the breathing a little uneasy, though he had to admit he wasn't minding the warm weather.

He went down to MWA headquarters, where Betty Rafferty was busy at her typewriter as usual. "Well, Barney, back from the great Midwest?"

"Yeah. I'm back. What's been doing here?"

"I've got a load of messages for you. One from Skinny Simon. He wanted to know if he can have lunch with you today if you got back in time."

Barney glanced at his watch. It was not yet eleven. "Sure, I could probably see Skinny. What about? Did he say?"

"No."

"What else?"

She mentioned a few routine MWA matters. He listened restlessly and then said, "Betty, could you check on some people and find out just where they were last Friday when I was in the Midwest?"

"Oh? You sound like a detective now."

He ignored the sarcasm. "And also, I want to know something about their background—anything you can find. People that were on Skinny's show that night. Max Winters, for instance. Has he gone back to California?"

She frowned at that. "I . . . I don't know, Barney. He was supposed to go back last week."

"What's that supposed to mean?"

"Nothing at all. What do you think I run—a gossip column here? Look, talk to your friend Susan Veldt. She probably can tell you where Max is."

"Then he is somewhere?"

"I don't want to say, Barney. After all, he is one of our Edgar winners."

He studied her closely, watched while she reached for a cigarette and lit it. It was the same sort of motion that Susan Veldt sometimes used—a very feminine motion, which he'd never really noticed before in Betty Rafferty. Maybe that was his trouble—that he never really had noticed it.

"Look," he said, "this thing between Susan and me is strictly business. What's the trouble?"

"No trouble. I just said you should go to her for your information. Not to me."

"Betty, we've known each other a long time. We've worked together. You've been like my right hand ever since I've had this executive vice presidency. What's bugging you now?"

She sighed and blew out a cloud of smoke. "If you must know, Barney, I think that girl's making a fool of you. She's making a fool of the whole organization. Have you been reading these things?" She tossed a copy of *Manhattan* to him.

The issue had come out while he was in the Midwest. Now he read it. It was still too soon for more than the briefest mention of the murder, but what there was was bitingly satiric. He stopped after a few sentences and tossed the magazine back on her desk.

"She didn't write this, her editor did."

"Barney, some of the people think you're being taken for a ride. They wanted you to look into the murder. They authorized you to look into it. They didn't authorize you to spend a long weekend hopping around the country with some girl reporter, sleeping with her, and heaven knows what else."

"You're sounding like a jealous wife or something," Barney said. "For your information, we were back Saturday."

She turned away, perhaps hiding the beginning of tears. He realized he had gone too far. Somehow he'd overstepped the bounds of propriety that had always existed between them.

"All right, Betty. All right. I appreciate your telling me. Where's this message from Skinny Simon? Is this his phone number here?"

She nodded, not speaking.

He called Skinny and confirmed the luncheon date at a French restaurant uptown, just off Madison. They would meet there at one.

He turned to say a few words to Betty, but she had stepped into the washroom. There was no sense waiting for her. She was obviously prepared to stay there till he left.

"Bye, Betty!" he yelled through the door. "I'll be back this afternoon for the board meeting." Then he went quickly down the stairs to West 48th Street.

Skinny Simon was waiting for him when he arrived at the restaurant, standing under a stylized sign that showed a swan pierced by an arrow. Some old French symbol, probably, that Barney didn't know. He'd been to the place before and liked it, but had never learned how to pronounce its name correctly.

They took a table in the rear and ordered more than Barney usually ate for lunch. Then, over a preliminary drink, Skinny leaned forward. "How are things going with the investigation, Barney?"

"As well as could be expected, I guess. You know how these things are."

"Word is you got shot at out in the Midwest. Nebraska? They still carry guns and ride horses out that way?"

"No, it was just some foolishness on my part. No damage done, except to the car I'd rented."

Again Skinny pulled back his lips and clicked his teeth together, in an annoying gesture Barney had noticed before. "We got pretty good ratings on the show last week. We might do another one. Same sort."

"Fine."

"Maybe we could do a show when you catch the murderer, huh?"

Barney shrugged. "Work it out with the cops."

"Has that detective been around?"

"Note lately." Barney lit a cigarette. "Where'd you hear I got shot at? I didn't think it was common knowledge yet."

"The girl mentioned it— Susan Veldt. I stopped by her apartment yesterday."

"Oh? What for?"

"She impressed me. I wanted to line her up for a future show."

"And pump her about the case," Barney said. "The same as you're trying with me."

"Gee, Barney. I was just hoping that over lunch you might open up a bit, tell me how things are going."

"Skinny, I couldn't do that. You're a newsman, of sorts. You'd probably have it on tonight's show."

"Oh, I don't do that sort of news. I'm just interested, that's all."

He remembered his request of Betty Rafferty to get information on people. He'd never gotten any further than Max Winters. "Skinny, have you seen any of the people who were on the show? Did you see any of them on Friday?"

"No. I'm seeing you now. Who else?"

"I was just wondering. Max Winters, especially. Has he been around town?"

"Thought he went back to California."

"Well, I thought he did too. I was just trying to make sure." He had another thought. "What do you do, a show every night?"

"Except for a few that we tape in advance occasionally, and the repeats. I work radio five nights a week, all but Friday and Saturday. Friday's the TV show. We all get sick occasionally, though."

"Were you sick last week?" Barney asked.

"Last week? No. Nobody gets sick in May. Why are you asking?"

Barney sipped some more of his drink. It burned going down. "I think one of the people on your show the other night might have followed me out to Nebraska and taken those shots at me. I'm just trying to sort out where people were. I guess I certainly couldn't have been you, could it? If you did your TV show."

"Did you really think it was me?" Skinny asked, looking horrified. "Do you think I go around killing people now, in addition to everything else? What's with you, Barney? You're not even trusting old friends."

Barney didn't bother to point out that Skinny had never been an old friend of his. "Of course," he said, "you might have taped your Friday TV show in advance, and had off the whole weekend."

"You're serious about this, aren't you? Do you seriously think that I killed Ross Craigthorn?"

Barney changed his tone to a laugh. "Not really, Skinny. Don't worry. I am interested, though, in knowing where some people are in this town. You don't know about Max Winters. How about Dick McMullen, the agent?"

"McMullen? Yeah, I saw him the other day. Forgot all

about him."

"Just thought I might take a run down to the Village and see him."

Skinny's eyes narrowed. "You know about McMullen, don't you?"

"What's there to know?"

Skinny shrugged. "If you don't know, I guess there's nothing to know."

"Come on, cut out the games! What should I know about McMullen?"

"Some people say he fools around with his authors. Not just the ladies, either."

"Oh?"

"It's talk. Just talk. Who knows?"

Barney had a sudden memory of McMullen with his arm around Max Winters's shoulder that night at the dinner. "Look, Skinny, it's late. I've got to be getting alone. Why don't you get to the point, if there is one? Then I'll be saying goodbye."

"No point, Barney. No point at all. It's just that I'd like an inside track when this case breaks, that's all. I know you're pretty friendly with that magazine gal, and I'd hate to think of her beating me to a scoop."

"I'll keep you in mind, Skinny," Barney told him.

The food arrived then, and the talk shifted to casual pleasantries. In another half-hour Barney excused himself and left Skinny at the table.

He called back to MWA headquarters, hoping that Betty had returned from lunch. She had. "Betty, this is Barney. Now look, I'm sorry for whatever I said."

"There's nothing you need to be sorry about, Barney."

"Okay. Now you made a few hints about Max Winters and I want to get to the bottom of that. Is Max still in town?"

"Yes," she said softly.

"Is he down at Dick McMullen's apartment in the Village?"

"I've heard talk."

"Okay. That's all I wanted to know. Look, Betty, they're a couple of adults. There's nothing you can do about it, so just forget it, huh? I'll go down and have a talk with Max."

"All right, Barney."

He hung up and caught a cab. This was not the sort of thing he usually did. But if talk had reached Betty Rafferty, it might have reached some columnists, too. It wouldn't look good, not a week after Max won the Edgar. He knew Max had a wife and family somewhere out west and he was sorry now that he didn't know more about them—and more about Max's particular problems, whatever they might be.

Dick McMullen answered the door on his second ring. It was a fancy apartment, very much in the Greenwich Village style, with desk and filing cabinets and all the trappings of a literary agent's office. A modernistic statue of a pair of lovers occupied one corner.

McMullen was lounging in a short robe, holding an icy drink in his hand. "You're just in time for afternoon cocktails, Barney. Good to see you again."

"Thanks, Dick. I've come on business."

"What kind of business would that be?"

"Max Winters. Have you seen him?"

"Max? Sure! He's here now, in fact!" Dick smiled. "Max! Come out! A friend of yours to see you!"

Max Winters appeared from the kitchen, carrying his own drink, fully clothed. Even to a suitcoat that seemed somewhat unnecessary. "Hi, Barney. How was the trip?"

"It was a good trip, Max. I'm surprised to see you here, though. I thought you'd be heading back to California."

"Dick and I had some business affairs to straighten out. He's going to be handling my next novel."

"I'm glad to hear that."

McMullen moved over to his desk, setting the drink on its edge. "Barney, something's bugging you! What's the trouble?"

"I'd like to talk to Max alone, if I could."

"Sure, go ahead. Be my guest."

Max downed his drink in two quick gulps that reddened his face. "I was about to leave anyway, Barney. I'll go with you."

Barney nodded. "Be seeing you around, Dick."

McMullen sat down behind the desk, saying nothing. The mask of hospitality had slipped away.

In the street, Barney said to Max, "How long are you going to stick around here?"

Max looked sideways at him. "Is it really any business of yours, Barney?"

"I just thought we were friends, that's all."

"We are. This is a personal thing, though."

"I know. And believe me, it doesn't make a bit of difference to me how you lead your life. But the word's getting around town. You just won the Edgar last week, and I'd like to avoid any bad publicity if I could. We've got enough already with the murders."

Max shrugged his weary shoulders. "Dick and I have been friends for years. He's my agent. What's so wrong with that?"

"Nothing, Max," Barney said. "Nothing at all. I guess I shouldn't have come down."

And he realized that he shouldn't have. Max was his friend, and that was all that mattered. "Forgive me for sounding like a father, or uncle or something."

Max's old smile returned. "You're forgiven, Barney. Don't worry about it."

Chapter Twenty-One

SUSAN VELDT

She sat in her usual chair opposite Arthur Rowe's massive desk, long legs crossed, smoothing the nylon over her knees. While she waited for him, she studied the shape of her legs beneath the short skirt, and decided they were pretty good. She decided she was pretty good, too. And decided for the tenth time since Saturday that she could have Barney Hamet any time she wanted him. The problem was just deciding whether she really did want him or not.

Then Arthur Rowe was back in the room and her thoughts were jerked into the present. He sat down, tossing a pile of new galleys onto the work table behind him, and faced her. "Tell me all about the trip. Tell me all about June, Nebraska."

"There's nothing much to tell that's not in my rough draft, and that's in the usual place."

"You got shot at! My secretary told me that much!"

"Not me. Barney. This is getting to be more than I bargained for, Mr. Rowe. Frankly, I don't know as I want to go on."

"Are you scared?"

"No, not scared. It's just more than I bargained for. I started out being some sort of spy for the magazine, gathering all this material for a great series on how MWA cracked or didn't crack their own murder case. Now somewhere along the line I've gotten caught up in it. Now I really do want Barney to find the killer. I want it for him, not for us, not for the magazine."

He looked pained. "Is that the sort of girl I've trained? Is that the sort of girl I've got working for me?"

"I'm afraid so. Maybe it has something to do with being a woman."

"Are you in love with the guy?"

"Nothing you could call by that name, no. But I think he trusts me. I don't know why he should. Certainly I've given him nothing but grief since we met. But . . . he trusts me, and somehow I should repay that trust. Somehow I should help him if I can. Not for *Manhattan*, or even for you, Mr. Rowe. But for him."

"What are you trying to tell me? That you want off the assignment?"

"You've got all week before your deadline," she said.

"I'll finish off this week. He's meeting with the board of directors this afternoon, and you'll have a full report on it. After that, I think you'd better get someone else."

"All right. If that's the way you want it."

"I guess it is. If you want me to, I'll submit my resignation."

"No, no," he said quickly. "You're too good a girl to lose. I'll put you on something else. The Pulitzer Prizes are being announced today. Maybe we can go back to the series idea that we originally planned. Actually, this murder is something of a nine-day wonder anyway. If there are no new developments by next week, it'll be a dead issue like everything else. And why should we beat a dead horse? I thought it might be sort of fun to do these articles, but I guess the fun has gone out of it. For you, at least."

"It has, Mr. Rowe."

"Right." He took out his pipe and carefully filled the bowl. "Then what else is there to say? If anything breaks at the directors' meeting this afternoon, though, I'd still like first crack at it."

"You'll have that," she said. "And thank you."

She left him alone and went back to her own desk, scanning briefly over the morning mail. Yes, she'd done it, and she'd done it for Barney.

Now what did that tell her about herself?

Chapter Twenty-Two

BARNEY HAMET

Barney faced the directors of Mystery Writers of America at four o'clock that afternoon. The directors' meetings were always held before the monthly meetings, but this one was an exception, called to review Barney's progress and the most recent events. He was aware, looking at them, at their drawn faces and not-so-casual joking, that this was indeed a crisis for the organization.

Perhaps they'd gotten into it too deeply by offering him the assignment in the first place. Perhaps they should have sat it out on the sidelines, waiting until the police came up with something more definite. With only the police investigating the case, they would be off the hook, whether or not the case was solved. But the press clamor on that first day had been too much for them. The murder at the MWA dinner had to be solved by MWA.

And so here he was, feeling not at all like an ex-private detective, or even like a present mystery writer—feeling just a little bit lost, with a lot of odds and ends of evidence. Now knowing exactly where to go from here.

He saw Susan Veldt enter late, just as the meeting was starting, and slip into a chair near the door, right next to Betty Rafferty. One or two of the directors eyed her unhappily, but no one made the move to oust her. They seemed to feel that she was there as Barney's guest, and perhaps she was.

"All right," he said, looking down the table, seeing Max Winters at the far end, with Hal Masur and Herbert Brean and the others. Harry Fox was there again, too. No one objected to Harry. He was part of the organization.

"All right," he repeated. "Now it's time to get down to business. A lot has happened this past week. Most of it, you know about. There's been a second murder—a woman named Irma Black. And her killer has even taken a couple of pot shots at me out in Nebraska. I found out a great deal about him. I know the motive for the killing. For both killings. And I can name the murderer. However, naming him and finding him are not exactly the same thing.

"This is the way it was. Ross Craigthorn, under the name of Craig, was brought up in the town of June, Nebraska. Irma Black also lived near June, though she worked across the state line, at a bank. She was a teller there. Craig, or Craigthorn, attended the University of Texas after he got out of the army. At the end of his second year, in 1947, he traveled up to June with a friend, a fellow named Victor Jones. I haven't been able to discover much else about Jones. The college yearbooks don't have any pictures of him, and he never graduated. The only snapshots we've come up with were blurred and no good for purposes of identification twenty-two years later.

"In any event, Victor Jones apparently was a wild sort. He and Ross Craigthorn adopted the names of Raven and Caesar respectively, for reasons I haven't yet determined. I suspect they engaged in some petty crimes, but the one crime that concerns us was in July of 1947, when they robbed the bank where Irma Black worked. Victor Jones walked in with a shotgun, held up the bank, and took Irma along as a hostage, while Ross Craigthorn waited outside in the car. It's not clear how much Craigthorn was actually involved in the planning, but he was certainly an accessory.

"They took Irma somewhere, held her prisoner for a week. I have a strong suspicion it was not entirely against her will. In any event, she was finally released, and claimed not to have been harmed. Some time later, two brothers—the Clancy brothers—were killed at a police roadblock, and blamed for the robbery, partly on Irma Black's testimony. She married a farmer, and led a fairly ordinary life for the next couple of decades, till just recently.

"Her husband died, and she came to New York to blackmail Ross Craigthorn over the past events. He was famous now, and although he could no longer be tried for that old crime, she apparently felt that she could ruin his reputation. She asked for one hundred thousand dollars to keep quiet. Of course even for Craigthorn this was out of the question. And I suppose he felt he'd matured enough to think he could throw himself on the mercy of the public.

"He'd chosen the opportunity of the MWA dinner to reveal his connection with the bank robbery. I suppose he even figured he could pay back the thirty thousand dollars that was stolen from the bank, if necessary. It would have been a good public relations gesture, and it would have been a lot cheaper than paying Irma Black a hundred thousand.

"Anyway, he must have told Victor Jones that he had this in mind. Jones could not, or would not, risk the revelation, perhaps because he could still be tried on a kidnapping charge. He killed Ross Craigthorn at the very moment he was about to tell his story. Why didn't he kill him sooner? Well, I suppose murder comes hard to any man the first time. Jones probably waited until the last possible moment, until he was sure that Craigthorn was going to reveal it. That's why he used that somewhat bizarre device to fire the bullet.

"After that, he thought he was safe, but of course Irma Black was still in town, and she sent a telegram to Skinny Simon's radio show, claiming to have information. Jones showed up and killed her. Just as Jones followed Miss Veldt and myself to Nebraska, and tried to kill me, after breaking into our car and stealing the one photograph of him that we had."

"Who is this Jones," Max Winters asked.

"Well, that's the problem. He's someone that was at the

MWA dinner. He's someone, I think, that was on Skinny Simon's radio show."

Harry Fox let out a short gasp. "One of us, you mean? Max—or me?"

"Not at all, Harry. There were a lot of other people involved in the show. I base that on the fact that the killer knew about Irma Black's telegram. He couldn't have found her any other way. I saw the letter that Irma wrote to Ross when she arrived in New York. She didn't mention any address. I don't think he ever knew where she was living. And therefore he couldn't have passed the knowledge on to Jones, whoever he is."

"Could Jones be someone in broadcasting," Harry asked.

"You mean like Skinny Simon? Sure, it's a possibility. And it's one that I haven't neglected. I've been very busy today. Just before this meeting, I had a talk with Betty, and she's trying to get information on the background of certain MWA members, and others like Skinny. Of course it's difficult, because we never send out any sort of biographical sheet, but she's been able to pick up a certain number of things.

"Max, your book jackets carry the statement that you went to UCLA and that your home is in California. But I suppose the real Victor Jones would have wanted to cover up his early days. He wouldn't want to mention the University of Texas or June, Nebraska, or any of the rest of it, so as not to be linked with that early robbery. We think Jones came to New York, and lives here now, but he could be someone who comes here occasionally and has access to an apartment here."

"Why an apartment?" Betty asked from the end of the table.

"There was a certain amount of work necessary in preparing the device that killed Craigthorn—drilling the cartridges and such. I don't think it could have been done in a hotel room."

Max Winters shifted uneasily and scratched at his beard. "What sort of information is Betty after?"

"Well, she's checking over the three hundred dinner guests. Just on the off-chance one of them might not have

167

covered his tracks. I've assembled all the information to pass on to Detective George. Probably it's best to work through the police. In fact, George is coming here later this afternoon to talk to me about it."

"Then you really have nothing conclusive," Harry Fox said, stating the obvious.

"I think we have enough so the police can get on it now. There might have been some other clues in that bank robbery. There might have been something in the files of the University of Texas. Jones left a pretty broad trail in those days, and even though it ended, for all practical purposes, in 1947, there must be some way of linking him with somebody in the present. That's what we've got to do."

"What about Raven?" Harry asked. "You called me on that from Nebraska. Anything new?"

Barney shook his head. "Raven is the biggest mystery of all. Craigthorn was obviously telling us, when he broke that statuette, that Raven was his killer. Victor Jones is Raven, we know that much. Just as Ross Craigthorn was Caesar in those early days. They were names that young men chose. Not boys exactly, because they'd both had army service, or at least Ross had. They were names picked from somewhere, and I've been trying to decide just what was in their minds at the time."

"Well," Max Winters said, "I vote that we allow Barney to continue his investigation. I think he's made great progress for just one week, and we all owe him a debt of gratitude."

"Sure," Harry chimed in. "Even if we get no further, just this evidence you've gathered and this name of Victor Jones is enough to convince the public that we've been doing a job on it.

"You can stay on the case, Barney. But I agree now that it's a matter for the regular authorities. We've come up with a lot more information that the police. Let them hunt out Victor Jones."

"Except," Barney reminded them, "that if he is a member of our group, if he is one of those people that was on Skinny Simon's radio show last week, I feel we have to get to the bottom of it ourselves."

The office door opened hesitantly, and they saw Detective George peeking around the corner.

"Come in," Barney said. "We're just finishing up here. I was giving the fellows a report on our progress so far, and I'll give the same report to you."

"Good. Glad to hear it," George told him.

The meeting broke up, and the members of the board drifted into small, chatty groups. Barney took George aside and spent the next twenty minutes filling him in on what he'd learned. The detective was interested, but beneath his interest there seemed to be a twinge of annoyance at Barney's efforts.

"We could have found this all out," George said, when he'd finished. "It might have taken us a little time, but we are equipped for investigations outside the city, you know."

"I know. Sometimes you get lucky in these things."

"Like back in the old private detective days, huh?"

"I never got this lucky then. Never investigated murder cases, either."

He left the detective and walked over to Susan. "How's it going today?"

"Fine. I told my boss that this was my last week on the big MWA murder case."

"Oh? Why is that?"

"I think you know why, Barney. I guess I've gotten too close to the thing. Something like that. Too close, not far enough away. I can't look at it objectively any more. I guess I see you, and some of these other people I've gotten to know, and I wish you luck. I don't just hang around for a story any more, like I did in those first few days."

"Glad to hear that," he said, leaning down to squeeze her hand. "Maybe there's hope for you yet."

"Barney, could I see you a minute?"

He turned at Harry Fox's voice, and walked over to the bookcase. Most of the others were drifting out. He waved to Max Winters and called to Betty Rafferty. "I'll lock up, Betty. You can take off for dinner if you want."

"Thanks, Barney."

"How's it going?" Harry asked.

"Good, good. Like I said before, we don't have anything

on the Raven business yet. We're still hoping."

As he talked, his eyes were scanning the titles behind Harry's head. They were in more or less alphabetical order, but occasionally one slipped out. *The Complete Sherlock Holmes* by Arthur Conan Doyle. *The Eighth Circle* by Stanley Ellin. Something by Margaret Erskine, its faded jacket hiding the title. A few Ian Fleming books, although he'd never been a member. Lots of Erle Stanley Gardner. Dorothy Gardiner, a former executive secretary. *Seconds* by David Ely, badly out of order. He flipped it off the shelf and stuck it up above.

"What was it, Harry? What did you want to see me about?"

"I thought I should tell you before you found out somewhere else. I'm a graduate of the University of Texas."

Dusty jackets and shelves. He'd have to speak to Betty about it.

"Oh?"

"I went there after the war. Just about the period you would have been talking about."

Barney blinked. "Ever know a fellow named Victor Jones?"

"No. Never did. Of course, we had a big enrollment. Thousands, even in those days."

"Or Ross Craig?"

"No. Didn't know him, either."

"Coincidence, I guess," Barney said. "I'm glad you told me about it, though. I might have gotten a little suspicious if I'd come across it somewhere."

He glanced across the room, toward where Susan was still waiting, then back at the books, Anthony Gilbert, Michael Gilbert, Winston Graham. All English authors. All very good. The publishers had donated the books to the MWA library, even though they weren't members.

"Did you get much of a look at the fellow who shot at you?" Harry asked.

"Just someone with a beard . . . funny . . ."

"What?"

"Funny. I just happened to think who he reminded me of."

"Who was that?"

"At the dinner. I was up on the speakers' rostrum, getting ready to introduce Craigthorn, and there was a fellow with a beard near the back of the room. I remember noticing him, not thinking much about it. I remember not recognizing him at the time . . . And you know, Harry—I really think it might have been the same person."

"Then Victor Jones could have been an outsider? A wolf in sheep's clothing?"

"You remember what happened to that wolf in Aesop? The farmer thought he was a sheep and killed him for food. Maybe the same sort of thing will happen to our murderer."

Barney's eyes stopped at another title. *The Third Man* by Graham Greene. A slim book. It had originally been a short story and was expanded to novella length to tie in with the motion picture version. A very popular movie in its day. Orson Welles . . . and somebody playing the zither. *The Third Man Theme.* Harry Lime. It had been a television series too. Harry Lime. Harry Fox. Barney reached out and touched the shelf.

"My God! The third man! The third man!"

"What . . . what is it, Barney? What third man? I thought you just got through telling us there were only two of them."

"What do you know about Graham Greene?" Barney asked. "About the names of his characters?"

Harry scratched his graying temple. "Well, I'm not much on modern authors. I can tell you a bit about some of his books, though. About *The Third Man*, for example. The character of Holley was called Rollo in the book version, but Greene changed it because Joseph Cotton—who played the part in the film—thought the name Rollo sounded like a homosexual."

Barney checked the copyright date. "But it wasn't published, even in its short version, till 1949. I need something earlier . . ."

"What's all this thing with names?"

Barney was pawing through the bookcase, but the volume he wanted was not there. He was almost certain—almost—that his memory wasn't playing tricks on him. He looked around for George, but the detective had already gone.

"Susan, are you waiting for me?"

"I was, Barney."

"Come with me, then. I have to make a stop at the public library."

"What is it?"

"I have to check on something. Something I should have seen a long time ago."

"But what?"

"Craigthorn's dying message.. We were fooling around with ravens—Poe's raven and Dickens's raven. But all the time we had the wrong raven."

It didn't take him long at the library. The book he wanted was in, and he only had to glance at page one to know the answer. It could have been one of the other books, but his memory had served him well. He'd reread them not too long ago, and he'd always been a fan of Graham Greene.

"Come on," he said to Susan. "I think I've got it. It's fantastic and improbable, but I think I've got it."

"You know who the killer is?"

"I know," he said. "I know the identity of Victor Jones. I know all there is to know."

"Barney . . ." She stood very close to him. "Barney, I promised Mr. Rowe something. I promised that he could have the information if I learned anything today—or this week, in time for his deadline. I'd like to keep that promise if I could."

Barney thought about it. "This thing belongs to the police. But if you want your boss in on it, I won't stop you. I'd like to meet him, in fact."

He went to a pay phone and called Detective George. "Look, I hate to get you out again. I know you're probably going home."

"Right. Home to supper."

"Give me an hour, and I think I can wrap this thing up. It's not quite five yet. We're on our way to the offices of

Manhattan magazine. Susan promised her boss a news break on the story."

"We don't give breaks to anyone. Not till the murderer is apprehended," George barked over the telephone. "If you've got something, you tell me first!"

"Play along with me. You won't be sorry."

"You mystery writers! You think this is all a game, don't you? Two people have been killed. You were shot at yourself."

Barney sighed, and spoke a few more words into the telephone. He didn't know if they were convincing words, but at least they quieted the detective down. He agreed to meet them.

"Do you really think you've got it, Barney?" Susan said in the cab. "Who is Victor Jones?"

"I think I've got it. The more I think about it, the surer I am. The pieces all fit together. They all fit together like a neat, neat jigsaw puzzle, and there's no other answer for it. The rest of it is up to the police. I'm not apprehending anybody. Not these days."

"You didn't answer my question."

"What?"

"Who is it? Who is Victor Jones? I'll admit I have my own ideas."

"Oh? Let's hear them."

So, settled back against the worn leather of the taxi seat, he listened and she talked. "I know you're not going to like this, Barney, but I think it's Harry. Harry Fox."

"Oh?" he said again.

"I heard him tell you he attended the University of Texas. And the rest of it just fits in too well. Victor Jones made his appearance out in June the night after you phoned Harry. It was Harry who was at all the board meetings, knew what was going on every minute. And even his name—Fox. The only animal name, the only name anything like Raven."

Barney only stared out the window, saying nothing.

"Well? Am I right?"

He smiled at her. "You'll know soon enough. Here's your office."

Detective George was waiting for them in the downstairs lobby. They fought the tide of five o'clock traffic streaming from the elevators and caught an elevator to the *Manhattan* offices.

"This way," Susan said as they left the elevator. Barney and the detective followed her through the plain brown reception area, then back along a lengthy corridor.

Arthur Rowe looked up as they entered, then set his pipe down carefully in the ash tray. "Susan! What's this?"

"I promised you a story, Chief. Here it is. Barney Hamet, Detective George, this is Arthur Rowe, editor and publisher of *Manhattan* magazine."

They shook hands all around. "Does this mean a break in the case?" Rowe asked.

"The last break," Barney told him. "It's a pleasure to meet you after all this time. I've heard a great deal about you."

Rowe nodded. "And I about you. We seem to share the affections of this young lady, in a purely literary sense, of course. On my part, at least."

They settled into chairs in a semicricle around the desk, and Barney began. Three pairs of eyes were on him, and he couldn't meet any of them. He looked out the window at the side of Rowe's desk, studying the view up Fifth Avenue. He had always liked tall buildings. The taller you were, the more important it all seemed, somehow. Maybe that's why magazines like *Manhattan* were always located high in the clouds.

"This won't take too long," he said.

Rowe thumbed through some galleys. "I have the rough copy for next week's article here, based mainly on the things that Miss Veldt wrote. We'd like a nice lead, naming the murderer."

"And I'll oblige," Barney told him. "The murderer is a man named Victor Jones, who was known to himself, and one or two others, as Raven. This was during a short period of his career, when he robbed a bank."

"And?" Arthur Rowe said. "That much I gather from Susan's reports. Are you prepared now to put a name to this Victor Jones or Raven character?"

"I am," Barney said. "For you, and for Miss Veldt, and for Detective George here."

The detective stirred in his chair, and Susan's eyes widened, as if at last sensing the final act.

Barney cleared his throat, and continued. "Victor Jones became Raven, and after that, he came to New York. He was quite successful here, under the name he uses now. Under the name of Arthur Rowe."

There was a gasp of disbelief from Susan, and Barney hurried on. "No fast moves please, Mr. Rowe, I think Detective George has a gun on you."

Chapter Twenty-Three

VICTOR JONES

He had not moved his hand toward the drawer, because he kept no gun there. He had not moved toward anything, really. It was just a start. A startled, sudden beating of his heart. They were here, facing him. Facing him with the truth. A truth they could not possibly know. And yet, they had named him. They had named him, and it had been for nothing. All for nothing!

He heard his voice answering. "That's the most fantastic thing I've ever heard!" he said. "You two gentlemen had better get out of my office at once. And, Susan, if you value your job, you'll see that they leave right now!"

"We have evidence," Barney Hamet said. "And we can get a great deal more. It's one thing trying to trace some three hundred-odd people back to Victor Jones and June, Nebraska. But it'll be a hell of a lot easier digging into your past. Seeing where it stops."

"You are really serious about this?"

"I'm really serious," Barney said. He sat there across the desk, intense, sure of himself, and Victor Jones, knew he should have killed him that night in the parking lot in June. "If you don't think so, just listen. Once I got on to it, everything fell in place. It was just like a row of dominoes toppling over. You see, one of the things that bothered me all along was Irma Black's murder. I was convinced one of the people on the program must have done it. Skinny Simon, or one of us panelists. Because who else would have known that she sent me the telegram? And asked me to come see her?

"But then I began to puzzle about that, too, and it didn't make any sense. Because certainly anybody in the studio, fearing Irma Black would tell all, would not have waited until after the noon appointment that I had with her. They would have gone to her place at once that morning, or certainly before noon. They would have made some effort to contact her—to kill her, to buy her off, to silence her in some manner.

"But what did the killer do? He came later. *After* Susan and I had been there. What could possibly be the reason for this? I can think of only one: he did not learn about the telegram sooner. He did not learn about Irma Black until some time late that morning. Too late to get down there before the noon meeting. And who was the only person we know that learned about the telegram late Monday morning? You, Mr. Rowe."

Victor's hands were sweating now, but this was a long way from proof. Let them try. Let them try to prove something.

"I had this knowledge?" he asked.

"You had this knowledge—because Susan told me on countless occasions that she typed up rough drafts of what took place in our investigation and left them in your *In* box each morning. It was for the continuing article she was writing about the killing. What it amounted to was that, each morning, on your desk, was a transcript of what had happened, what had gone before, what I'd been doing. No wonder you were so anxious for her to stick close to me and write this series!

"That morning, Monday morning, you read her report and learned about Irma Black."

Susan interrupted here a bit hesitantly. "He was in a meeting, and I left it on his desk! He was still in the meeting when I went down to meet you. It would have been some time later, probably about noon, before he read it."

"And then," Barney continued, "he wasted no time—did you, Mr. Rowe?" Mr. Rowe, Mr. Jones, Mr. Raven. You went down there and killed her, before she could do any more talking to anybody.

"The same holds true for our trip to Nebraska, of course. You knew all about it, right from the beginning. Susan even called to keep you abreast of developments. You knew just the time when you had to make the trip. You knew where to find us. You knew which car was ours, because Susan's flowery attaché case was in the back seat. I hadn't seen the attaché case before that day, and none of the others had seen it, either. Not at MWA. But you saw it every day in the office, didn't you? And you found us right away, and broke into the right car, even though there was an identical blue Ford parked right next to ours. No one but you could have identified our car from Susan's attaché case, Mr. Rowe."

"I think you'll need a lot more than that in court," Victor Jones said, holding his hands steady now. "A great deal more than that."

"I have more," Barney said. "I was at the MWA office today, and I happened to see a book—*The Third Man*, by Graham Greene. And I remembered Ross Craigthorn's murder, and the exact circumstances of it. You see, the gimmicky murder device with the bullet fired by a radio signal served more than one purpose. It tended to implicate a mystery writer by its very deviousness, but it did much more. It enabled the killer to wait in perfect safety until the last possible moment before firing that bullet, maybe with the faint hope that Craigthorn would change his mind and not reveal the secret after all. You must have stood there with your finger on the switch of that radio transmitter, ready to send a signal across the room to the podium, to fire the bullet from that tube."

"But Mr. Rowe wasn't even at the dinner!" Susan protested, seeming to grasp at a final straw. Her eyes had hardly left Victor's face since they entered.

"I'll get to that in a moment," Barney told her. "Right now I want to remind you of the instant Craigthorn was shot. I've already shown that the radio device made it possible for the shot to be fired at any instant, and that the murderer was standing there—at the back of the ballroom, as it happens—listening to the speech. Therefore he must have pressed that switch at a specific point in time—the point at which Ross Craigthorn started to talk about him.

"As soon as I decided this, I tried to think back to what Craigthorn was saying just as he was shot. He was talking about a young man he'd known in his youth. Both of them had started reading mysteries. He mentioned how the young man was especially fond of novels of intrigue written by Graham Greene. I thought about this, and I knew, of course, that the man he referred to must have been Victor Jones, because why else would the killer strike at that single instant in the talk? Victor Jones admired Graham Greene's novels, just as Ross Craigthorn had also admired mysteries.

"And when it came time for them that summer to pick some names, names of criminals, or heroes, or what have you, they chose the names of Caesar and Raven. Although we'll never know for sure, I feel certain that Caesar was from W. R. Burnett's popular novel and movie, *Little Caesar*, the classic gangster thriller of the thirties.

"And Raven? Where did Raven come from? Where would Raven come from? Thought up by a young man who admired Graham Greene's novels? Not the raven of Edgar Allan Poe, nor the raven of Dickens and Barnaby Rudge. No, it could only be the raven of Graham Greene. The hired killer who was the protagonist of *This Gun for Hire*, and who was known only by that name—Raven. There could be no doubt about this. And in telling me that Raven had killed him, perhaps Ross Craigthorn was trying to tell me something more. He had only an instant to live, and the Raven was the only thing handy. He felt that somehow this would be enough, and perhaps it was, in a way.

"You see, after Craig lengthened his name to Craigthorn and came east, Victor Jones—Raven—did the same. He came east too, But he didn't want Victor Jones for a name, and he couldn't keep Raven for one, much as he may have wanted to. Is it too unlikely that this fan of Graham Greene's books would search further in the novels for another name?

"It's not an easy thing to find a name in Graham Greene's crime novels. The protagonist of *The Confidential Agent* has only an initial, D., and the protagonist of *Brighton Rock* only a nickname, Pinkie. And *The Third Man* had not yet been written in 1947, of course. But is there another Greene novel in which he might have looked? Yes, there is. A couple in fact, if you count earlier ones like *Orient Express*. But I think perhaps the one that attracted him was *The Ministry of Fear*, in which the protagonist is a very bookish chap, with the name of Arthur Rowe."

They were all looking at him now, looking at him and knowing it was true. They weren't thinking of whether this kind of foolish evidence would hold up in a court of law. It was the sort of thing that convinced people. Susan, and the detective, and this fellow Hamet. They were looking at him and knowing it was true. That Victor Jones had become Raven, and Raven had become Arthur Rowe. Because of a name in a book, a long time ago.

"But I would have seen him at the dinner!" Susan argued again.

"That stopped me for a while," Barney admitted, "until I remembered where I'd seen the man with the beard who fired the shots at me. I'd seen him, or someone very similar, at the dinner when I was on the podium. I'd seen him standing near the back of the ballroom. And I wondered at the time who he was—what group he belonged to. The answer, of course, was that he belonged to no group. He had simply walked in, as I pointed out earlier that anyone could. He had walked in, wearing a beard as a disguise. Because of course you would have known him, Susan. And certainly others in the publishing world would have recognized him too. Craigthorn never noticed, of course. He was just one more person, and the beard was a good enough disguise for his brief presence there.

"Once I decided that the killer had entered the ballroom wearing a disguise, it put a whole new aspect on the case. It proved, to me at least, that the killer was not one of the three hundred invited guests, nor one of the waiters, or someone associated with the hotel. Because none of these people would have needed a disguise. The killer was someone from the outside. And again, all roads led to your boss, Susan. It was a perfect setup for him. By coincidence, he already assigned you to cover these various awards presentations. I imagine he had the MWA dinner date jotted in his notebook when Ross Craigthorn originally contacted him. So it was a simple matter to send you there and, when murder became necessary, to assign you to write the series."

He turned to Victor once again. "You didn't really care, of course, whether the articles made good copy or not. Your main interest was in following the course of my investigation, and you did that. You did it quite well, Arthur, or Victor. You had Susan giving you written daily reports of exactly what went on. That was all you needed to find Irma Black, and to follow us to Nebraska.

"There were a lot of other little things, of course. The man who shot at me in Nebraska dropped some cigarette butts. You're smoking a pipe now, but I see there are cigarettes on your desk too. So obviously you smoke both. Also, you're known to come originally from the Midwest, as did Victor Jones." He waved a hand in a gesture of climax. "I've already mentioned about Susan's flowered briefcase, and the rest of it."

"You'd better come along," the detective said quietly. "Just while we check your background. If you're innocent, sir, you have nothing to fear."

Victor Jones rose and came slowly from behind his desk. He was nodding his head. "Yes. Yes, certainly I'll come along. I have nothing to fear. These accusations are ridiculous! I never went to the University of Texas! I never did any of these other things you're talking about. I never robbed a bank! I never . . ."

But now he was coming around the side of the desk, and suddenly the window was there. A solid sheet of glass, protecting him against the outside world. "I never . . ." he began again.

And in that instant, it seemed the easy way out. The easiest way out. The only way out.

"Grab him!" Barney yelled, diving across the desk, upsetting the pipe rack and the cigarette box, scattering manuscript pages.

But it was too late. It was too late for any of them to reach him now. The window shattered under his weight, splinters of glass cutting into his skin. They had his jacket, but not enough to hold him. He felt it rip as he went into the air, away from them, free.

He had often wondered if it would be a hard thing to do. But now he knew it wasn't. As the pavement rushed up to meet him, he knew it was the easiest thing in the world.

Chapter Twenty-Four

BARNEY HAMET

"It was such a long way down," Susan said sometime later. Much later, a lifetime later. But only that night.

Barney finished his drink and ordered two more for them. They were in a little bar, somewhere off Fifth. He hadn't really noticed which one it was. They'd been in there a long time, ever since the police finished questioning them.

"It's always a long way down," he said. "For guys like Arthur Rowe."

"I still can't believe it, Barney. Sometimes he was almost like a father to me."

"It's over now. I hope you're not out of a job."

"I don't think I could go back there now. Not ever again."

"Maybe I can find you something around town," he said. "I still have a few connections."

She sipped her fresh drink, made a face and pushed it away. "Let's go somewhere, Barney."

"Like where?"

"Like up to my apartment."

"I was there once before. Remember?"

"That was a long time ago. That was with a different girl."

Barney nodded and signaled for the check. He'd always been one to take a chance, especially with a girl like Susan Veldt.